NO GUNS AT MY SON'S FUNERAL

Paro Anand runs a programme — Literature in Action — in Delhi and various places outside, including Kashmir. She is a performance storyteller and an actress. She works with children and has helped them make the world's longest newspaper in eleven languages in sixteen different states in India in the year 2000. This is her thirteenth book. She has been awarded for her contribution to literature.

NO GUNS AT MY SON'S FUNERAL

paro anand

IndiaInk
ROLI BOOKS

Indialnk

© Paro Anand 2005

First published January 2005
Second impression July 2005

Indialnk
An imprint of
Roli Books Pvt. Ltd.
M-75, G.K. II Market
New Delhi 110 048
Phones: ++91 (011) 2921 2271, 2921 2782
2921 0886, Fax: ++91 (011) 2921 7185
E-mail: roli@vsnl.com; Website: rolibooks.com
Also at
Varanasi, Bangalore, Jaipur

Cover Design: Sneha Pamneja
Page Layout: Narendra Shahi

ISBN: 81-86939-17-2

Typeset by Roli Books Pvt. Ltd. and
printed at Syndicate Binders, Noida - 201 305

To Mummy who has taught me
that you don't need perfect circumstances.
To Keshav, Aditi and Uday
my wisest friends,
my sukoon

ACKNOWLEDGEMENTS

To Lt Gen. and Vijaylakshmi Nagaraj for starting me off in the first place. Ratna Mathur and Rajiv Gandhi Foundation for reintroducing me to the children of Kashmir and confirming that I was on the right track. To the Charles Wallace Trust for *not* giving me the Residency, for it taught me not to wait for the perfect time and place, but to just write. Many Vasant Valley students who have encouraged me along, even if they do not know it. To all those who have read the book before it was published and given their valuable inputs – Arun, Shiv, Vidyun, Micro, Mrs Narang, Renuka, Nandita and my family. To Mama whose love for Kashmir binds me to it – and her. To my fathers, Daddy and Papa, whose strengths I lean on. To Bete, dear friend, painstaking editor – I thank you all for this baby being born.

In fact there didn't seem to be
Anything left for us to see
A shred, a shard, a tuft of hair
A flip-flop flung without a care
But the dust we scuffed
Beneath our feet
Revealed a blood-red underneath

– Paro Anand

1

*Aftab was in a tearing hurry, but he didn't
want to arouse his mother's suspicions*

Aftab was in a hurry, a tearing hurry. He knew that he
was already late. And he didn't want to be. Couldn't
afford to be. But, then, he couldn't arouse his mother's
suspicions either. She was one of the suspicious mother
types, who thought you were up to no good at all times,
even if it was an innocent swim in the Jhelum with his
friends. And that was another thing, she never approved
of his friends. 'They're not a good influence on Nooro,'
she repeated like a stuck record whenever his father was
about. Luckily, father was too preoccupied with his work
problems most of the time and was unable to pay much
attention to her. So now he had to sneak out of the house.
And sneak out in a hurry. There wasn't much time and he
knew that the meeting would start without him. Every
time he was late, it was a repeat of the last time, with
everyone laughing, 'Arre, ma ke lal, phir ma kee phiran

mein phas gaya kya?' – Still mama's precious little darling? And they'd all laugh. He hated that. He hated being laughed at. He wasn't the youngest, but unfortunately he was the shortest. Javed, who was only twelve, was almost a head taller and behaved as though he was older than Feroze and Akram even. Even though they were men now.

Aftab's mother finally sat down with her kahwa. She had stoked the fire, filled a kangri for each member of the family and now it was time for her to rest her swollen feet and massage them with warm mustard oil. He hoped and silently prayed that she would not ask him to do that for her tonight. Not tonight. He usually enjoyed this time with her. She would quietly talk to him about her long-ago childhood. About the way things used to be. Free and safe. Or she'd ask him about how things were now. Now when things were neither free nor safe. Now, when mothers wouldn't let their children out of their sight. Now, when there were rumours of atankvadis luring young boys away with the promise of money and martial arts training and weapons. Rumours, too, of them enticing young Kashmiri girls away to be their 'brides'.

But tonight, he wanted to make a getaway. For his friends would be waiting and the meeting would have started. Aftab held his breath as he crouched, in his warm phiran, by the darkened doorway. Hoping against hope that she would find it sufficient to massage her own feet. She didn't call. A minute passed and then another.

And he was out of the house. Easing the door behind

him. Then, like a bullet shot out of a gun, he was away. Streaking through the early frost towards the 'safe' house where the meeting was to be held tonight. Akram, whom Aftab admired like the older brother he didn't have, but longed for. Akram, so handsome, so tall, so sure of himself. So brave. Akram, who wore his battle scars like medals. Akram, who people said, was not a Kashmiri, but actually a firangi, a foreigner. Akram, who was the only one who never made fun of him, but made the others shut up when they laughed about the way he still listened to his mother, and feared his father. Akram.

'Akram …,' Aftab panted, as he hurtled in through the door, 'Akram Bhai, I'm sorry, maaf karna, der ho gayee.'

'Kya hua, maa ki god mein so gaya tha, kya?'

The others laughed as Javed mimed him asleep in his mother's lap, sucking his thumb.

'Arre rahne do,' said Akram in his commander's voice. And the others shut up. 'Aao, Aftab, der aye durust aye, kyon?'

Aftab shot him a grateful, adoring look, and the older man acknowledged it with a smile before returning to the business at hand. Javed had seen the exchange, though, he nudged Imran who sat next to him, and made a stupid kissy face, pointing at Aftab.

'Javed,' said Akram sharply, and Javed jerked to attention, dismayed at being caught. Imran smiled under his long dark lashes. He was like that, thought Aftab,

3

happy to have someone else in trouble, any one at all. Friend or foe.

And then it was time for their exercise. Akram was extremely particular that his little army was in peak physical condition. He made them stretch, jump and carry each other. He worked them hard, using sacks of rice for weight training. Working them till their muscles screamed and the room steamed with their sweat, no matter how cold it was outside.

Afterwards, it was back to their planning. 'The army has received its orders. The ceasefire is over now. They are going to be hot on our tails. We have to act fast.'

'We have to act now,' added Feroze, trying to light his next cigarette. He always lit one with the butt of the first. His hands shook as the butt went out before the next was lit. His lips trembled and the cigarette fell on his lap. 'If we can only find out when the next important visitor is coming to Baramullah, it will help us do something really sensational,' Akram explained as he casually picked up the dropped cigarette and handed it back to his partner. Then he struck a match and held it to the other's lips until the cigarette was lit.

Aftab looked at Akram's face in the flare of the match. It glowed golden. His eyes, deep green, seemed to dance with a fire of their own. One that matched the match. The gash that ran from the hairline to the right eyebrow was etched deep. On anyone else it would have been disfiguring. But on Akram, Aftab thought, it looked so grand. It added to his aura of a dashing warrior. Aftab could only see perfection when he looked at Akram. And he never looked deep enough to see the cracks, the imperfections that festered below.

The match sputtered out and the room was filled with its usual gloom. If only Imran and Javed would stop being so stupid, Aftab would have felt that life here was perfect, even though the danger that was the focus of their discussion today was real and immediate. Aftab noticed that Javed was staring at Feroze's trembling hands as they quietened in his lap. Akram noticed too and clucked in irritation. He was extremely protective of Feroze and knew that Feroze was self-conscious about his infirmity. Aftab wondered what had happened to make him so shaky. There were lots of stories, but there was no way of knowing which one was true.

The meeting continued. The plotting, the planning. Aftab loved it all. He felt like a big hero in the films. Like Hrithik Roshan in *Fiza*. He could easily picture Akram in that role. Cloaked in black, green eyes blazing out at those who hurt him. AK-47 in his powerful arms. Muscles rippling, jaws clenched, he could mow down a platoon of soldiers all by himself. Aftab tried to picture himself in a similar scene. But when the blood started to spurt, his stomach churned. Yes, even the thought of blood, warm and living, made his worst nightmares come alive. Thank God Javed hadn't discovered this little fact about him yet. After all, blood was an essential, integral part of what they were – freedom fighters, liberators. Or atankvadis, as others called them.

On Bakr Id last year, when Abba had called him to help with the slaughtering of the goat, Aftab had thrown up right on the poor animal, and worse, on his father's shoes. He'd got his ears painfully twisted for that. And had been at the receiving end of Amir's jokes. Luckily, his younger brother had been silenced by Ammi, otherwise the other boys in the school would have come to know, and then Javed and then, worse, worst of all, Akram ....

'So Aftab, kahan ho bhai, Jhelum mein dubkee laga rahey ho kya?' Akram's voice jolted the boy gently back to the present.

'Hain, nahin, I mean ... .' He trailed off lamely. There it was again, the two exchanging looks of glee at Aftab's discomfiture.

'Acha, dekho,' said Feroze taking over, 'We've got to make some inquiries. Our next operation has to be high profile. The big outfits have been hogging all the newspaper headlines. Frankly, we're getting sidelined. Now, while the forces are busy with crackdowns on the main guys, it's time to make our move.'

'Aftab, any ideas?'

'I, I don't ... well ... I'll look around, I'll think, um ... try ....'

'Imran?'

Imran was full of ideas, a wedding, an annual day celebration at a school, a hit at a temple on Diwali, or on a gurudwara on Guru Purab.

He shot a smug look at Aftab who, of course, felt immediately smaller, and more useless than ever. Akram took down notes, nodding, acknowledging the younger boy's ideas. Javed shifted uncomfortably. It was obvious that he had no original ideas of his own. Akram turned to him, 'Hain Javed, anything?'

'Er – I'm trying to find out something … there's a possibility, but, I have to find out, I'll let you know.' He bluffed his way through.

Now it was Akram's and Feroze's turn to exchange a look. They smiled. 'Good,' said Feroze, 'So let us know as soon as you've cleared things with your sources.' Imran grinned, today he had come out with flying colours and he knew it. And he knew the others knew as well.

Meeting adjourned, they got up. Aftab's heart was heavy. He always came out so weak and useless. Imran, so full of ideas; Javed, just to prove himself, would come up with something or the other by the end of the week. But Aftab, well, there were no bright ideas waiting to be released, no earth-shattering, war-winning strategies. He dawdled; let the two younger boys go ahead of him. He wasn't up to taking their barbs and jibes just now. When would he ever prove to be the hero he wanted to be, or had dreams of being? When would Akram Bhai's eyes rest on him in admiration, not amusement? He would do anything for that, anything at all ….

Feroze was lighting his next cigarette. Akram was putting away the 'stuff' under the old clothes in the dusty,

7

old chest. So that if there was a raid, nothing would be found.

'Shaba khair, Feroze Bhai, Akram Bhai,' said Aftab softly as he lingered, putting on his shoes, slipping his arms into the phiran, leaving the sleeves to dangle emptily by his side.

'Aftab – good.'

'Good?'

'Yes,' the green eyes sparkled with amusement, 'Sometimes it is wisest to hold one's tongue than blabber on when you have nothing to say.'

Aftab glowed. He was part of the inner circle. He was sharing a joke with the seniors. He. Not Imran, not Javed. He. He grinned happily and went on his way whistling.

'Ladka acha hai, kaam ka hoga,' said Akram turning to Feroze.

'Par abhi chota hai, abhi to chuuza hi hai,' argued Feroze. He himself had entered the jihad when he was about as old as Aftab was now. And he knew well the dangers of being 'persuaded' into doing something you weren't yet ready for. He often looked at the younger boys as no more than fluffy yellow chicks, squawking about, scratching for juicy bits to play with. No more. Just cute little chicks playing at being heroes. At such moments Akram would shake his head vigorously. 'Nahin, Feroze, you're wrong. One should never wait till these new recruits are old enough to start thinking for themselves. Then they lose courage, once they know what the dangers ahead of them are. You have to use them while their dreams are bigger than their knowledge. While they're still hypnotized by its romance, by the likes of you and me.'

'Arre Akram Bhai, abhi bacche hain, itnee bhi kya jaldi hai, they're just children, let them play their games, there's enough time for them to prove themselves as heroes.' Feroze's shaky hands were lighting up their next cigarette. Akram noticed that his hands were shaking even more. He was worried. He would have to be careful, if Feroze started becoming sympathetic towards the boys ....

2

*Last night everything was so perfect, now
everything was upside down*

The clink of teacups, the sound of the kerosene stove being fired up. The woodsmoke smell of kangris being freshened. Aftab awoke to the sounds and smells of familiar security. He lay in bed, snuggling into his blanket. It had been his father's. It still held his scent. The tobacco smell of the hookah, the mystery of long nights, the smell of outdoors and home, all mixed into the pressed fibres of the wool. Aftab waited for his mother to bring him his tea in bed. He loved this time. The time of rest and peace. Peace – ah!

Aftab waited. Amir was whining, wanting more sugar in his tea. Wanting more milk. Basically, wanting more attention. Always, wanting more attention from Ammi and Abba. He never waited for tea in bed. He was too impatient for it. He was one of those who could beat the sun getting up. Always restless, always moving, shaking, twisting. It was so irritating. Aftab waited. He knew that his mother would pour in more milk, spoon in more sugar for his little brother and then bring him his tea. He now heard Shazia, his sister, humming as she swept the front of the house. Her quiet humming was about the only sound she made; she'd become quieter these days. But Aftab didn't have time to worry about a woman's preoccupations. She was older than him and their parents were on the lookout for a groom for her. They had started early because brave young men who were not involved in the fighting were hard to find nowadays. And Ammi wouldn't hear of marrying her daughter to anyone who'd held a gun. For one side or the other. She was fanatical about it, violence made her sick. The smell of gunpowder and death were never to enter her home, she said. Hands that had cradled a killing gun would never rock her grandchild, she had promised. *She could say all she wanted to, no one would listen to her words and warnings until later. Much later.*

Aftab waited. His ears strained to hear the cause of the delay. Amir had stopped whining. He'd gone out to drink his tea and share his bakarkhani with the chicken. Aftab waited. What was keeping Ammi? He caught the sounds of his parents talking, but they were speaking too softly for him to hear the words. So he waited some more.

'Come on, lazy bones. Get up! Don't you remember, today's a bandh? No school today. Come on, let's play cricket. Harmeet and Angad are already playing in the maidan.' Amir was tugging at his bedclothes.

'Oh ho, let me be, Ammi hasn't even brought me my chai yet,' snapped Aftab, snatching his bedclothes back around himself.

'Bhai, Ammi isn't going to bring you your tea …,' whispered Amir.

'Why not?'

'I don't know, she's angry with you, she says that she's spoiling you and she's not going to do that anymore,' explained Amir in a conspiratorial whisper.

Aftab's heart sank. Oh no, had she found out anything? Had she discovered that he'd gone to the 'firangi's' house against her wishes? She was dead against her children or husband getting friendly with the Afghans and Pathans who hid amongst them all nowadays. 'They're not us, they're firangis. They don't want our good, they just want what's good for them. Don't fall into their trap,' she often warned. Aftab was growing tired of her constant nagging; most of all, he hated the way her voice would be edged with venom when she talked about the firangis. She was talking about men like Akram, and the boy couldn't bear that. Couldn't bear hearing ill about his mentor. Couldn't bear it that he couldn't stand up for him, but swallow his protests like a coward, instead. But for now, he knew that he had to win his mother's trust back. He knew how to do it, he knew her soft spots. Always look for your enemy's soft spots, vulnerabilities, Akram taught them, time and time again. He'd also impressed upon him that anyone who was not with 'the cause' was an enemy. Even if it was Ammi you were thinking about. If only Akram could see him now. He'd be proud, his Akram Bhai.

Aftab scrambled out of his sleep-warmed bed. He cursed under his breath as the chill bit into him. Really, his mother was becoming too much. Why couldn't she mind her own business? Besides, how was it that she got to know so much? She was in the house all day long. Then how did she know where he'd been? Sheepishly, all ready to apologize, fibs ready to roll off his tongue, ready to grovel a bit, if he had to, Aftab entered the kitchen. His mother looked up to see him. She pointedly turned her back to him.

'Good morning, Ammi, Abbu,' he began. Amir sniggered in the background. 'Serves him right,' thought Amir, 'He never takes me anywhere with him.' Abbu ruffled his hair and went out of the room to get ready.

'Ammi, chai nahin tayar hui?' Without turning around, Ammi put a glass of tea on the table beside her. Swallowing the lump of unease in his throat, Aftab went to her and put his arms around her shoulders. 'Oh ho, Ammi, you're very angry with me?' Her shoulders tightened, but she didn't move away. Teasingly, Aftab pulled at the corners of her headscarf. She clucked her tongue and ducked her head.

'Stop it, Noora,' she swatted his hand.

'Ah ha, kyun meri Ammi jaan aaj nakhre kar rahee hain ...?' He persisted, now tickling her neck. But he had picked a wrong moment.

Suddenly she stood up, towering above him, even though she was actually very short. Even shorter than him.

'Nakhre mein nahin – it's you, you – you spoilt brat who is playing, playing, I don't know what dangerous games. Allah khair kare, if something happens to you – you'll get us all into trouble!'

Abbu came rushing back into the kitchen. It wasn't often that he heard his wife's voice raised in anger. 'Kya hua?'

'Nothing, it's ... nothing,' Ammi shook her head, her anger spent.

'What is it – why were you shouting?'

'Rehney do, just, just let it be.'

But Aftab knew his father wasn't going to let it be. Like a dog worrying a bone he went on asking: what, why, how come? Aftab also knew that Ammi would be regretting her outburst. Knew that eventually, she'd have to tell Abbu and that Abbu would then let his hands do the talking. Aftab held his breath and waited for the inevitable to happen. It happened.

'It's, it's nothing ... Aftab went out of the house last night, after I'd told him not to ... I don't know ....'

A sharp cuff on his ear sent the young boy and his tea reeling. He was caught by surprise despite being prepared. Ammi screamed, Aftab yelped, Abbu shouted.

The blows rained hard when Abbu was angry. He simply lost all control. Aftab backed away, trying to save himself. He backed all the way, right out of the house. But still his father came after him, yelling, cursing, hitting, wherever he could find an unprotected spot.

It was only outside, when neighbours stopped in their little chores, stopped to stare at the young lad cowering, the older man towering, the mother begging for mercy for her son, that Abbu, with one final kick, stormed out of the gate, still cursing. Shazia, who'd also stopped, clucked her tongue and shook her head as she bent over the broom once more. Really, her brother could be so stupid, would he never learn ...?

Mother and son were both crying, seeking comfort in each other's arms. The show over, the neighbours went back to their work. The mother led her son back into the house. Apologizing to him, chastising herself, brewing fresh tea, warming the bakarkhani with sob-racked shaking hands. After the soothing kahwa, Aftab hid his head in his mother's lap. He could hear the shouts and cheers of his friends as they got on with their game of cricket. But right now, he revelled in his mother's touch, as she rubbed his slap-sore body. The roughness of her calloused hands, combined with the gentleness of her touch, magically erased the pain, eased the sting of humiliation from his heart. A warm tear fell on his forehead. Looking up, he saw that she was crying, face bent over his. 'I'm sorry,' she whispered into his hair, cradling him now. He bit back on the, 'I'm sorry too,' that arose in his throat. Akram had taught him how to use just such a moment well. 'Turn your opponent's weakness to your advantage, your weapon,' he had said. He turned his mother's guilt to his own advantage, now.

'Nooro, beta, you're young, you don't realize the dangers out there.' And then the ultimate mother's line, 'I do this for your own good, you know that don't you?'

'Ammi, Ammi, Ammi,' smiled Aftab, stroking her head as it rested on his broadening shoulder, 'Ammi, what I do, where I go, I can't tell you anything, but see, you must believe me. What we're doing, it's for the good of all of us. Yours, Abbu's, Shazia Aapa's, mine – but most of all, for the good of the little ones, like Amir.'

'But, beta, why do you go out in the dark? These are bad times. Allah khair kare, if the police, or the army, or the militants find you wandering about at night, you know what could happen? You could get into trouble, serious trouble. Do you know beta,' she dropped her voice, just in case her husband was listening. He was a good, hard-working honest man, he couldn't bear to see his son involved in all this. 'Do you know, beta, not only you, we would all be in trouble if the police or the army was to find you wandering around at night. They say they take away fathers of such boys, and no one hears from them again. You are young, just a child, you don't know what's going on out there. Someday, Inshahallah, things will change, go back to the way they were when I was a child. Free. Safe. Why, even a kuwari girl could go out in the dark. Every man was a brother – Hindu, Muslim, it didn't matter. There was a time when we were just Kashmiris. And that was enough. More than enough. We shared each other's food, danced at each other's festivals, wept at each other's sorrows. Religion did not matter, you just leaned on the nearest shoulder, wept on it, if you needed to. We had brothers around us all the time to help us, protect us. Now only death lurks. Not in dark corners, but in the open streets, in broad daylight. I wish it could be like the old days again. When we were surrounded by the people of our own biradari. Now, beta, you don't know who your enemy is. Kashmir is like a bird whose wings have been torn apart. I don't know if she'll ever fly again. Beta, there was no danger then. No firangis with evil intentions … firangis …!' she spat the word out like a curse, 'Firangis. They've ruined their homeland and now they're hell-bent on destroying our beautiful valley, our jannat.'

'Ammi,' snapped Aftab, pushing her away. He couldn't bear for even his mother to speak ill of Akram and his people. She just didn't understand.

'You just don't understand.' He faced her. 'They're not firangis, they are our own. They are our real brothers. They are helping us ….'

'They are helping themselves, Noora. They are helping themselves. To our money, homes, food and worse – to our peace of mind. They are driving stakes into the heart of this land that is ours. Don't you see that?' Her nails dug into the soft skin of his arm, emphasizing the urgency of her words. She knew that she had to get through to him, if she didn't do it now, it would be too late. *Way too late.*

'No. I don't. Ooof, Ammi, you don't know anything.' Aftab was trembling with rage. 'You – you stay inside the house and then pretend to know what's going on outside. You've been blinded by the propaganda. These people are not the outsiders here. It's the Indians, the army, the police. They're just puppets in the hands of the people in Delhi.'

Ammi's eyes were flashing with real anger now. 'And what exactly do you know about Delhi and the people there? Who's been filling your head with all this? And is your head so empty that you're willing to fill it with any garbage that comes your way? Do you know why our Kashmir has come to such a state? It's because of the people who have come from across the borders. Who have no iman of their own. No religion, no roots. They come here and sever the roots. Our roots, our children's roots. Cut them so deep that we'll all fall down one day. Khatam. Don't get mixed up with these dangerous people, Nooro, I'm warning you. If I find you playing these dangerous games, there'll be no one worse than me. I am warning you, your father's beatings will seem like caresses if I find that you've been mixing with them.'

'Oooof, it's useless talking to you, you'll never understand.' Slamming the door as hard as he could,

Aftab stormed out of the house. Shazia looked up, 'Aftab suno ...,' but he didn't want to listen to another woman's advice and lectures. What did she know? Even though she was eighteen, she was still a young girl, just a helpless woman. He continued walking. He hesitated outside the gate. Should he join his friends in their game of cricket, or should he go the other way, towards the bazaar?

'Chowka! It's a boundary!' Cheers and yells went up from the cricket field. But Aftab felt sick at heart. He wanted to be alone. Slipping his arms into his phiran sleeves, the boy determinedly turned his back on the happy voices and wandered towards the bazaar. Just now he wanted to be alone with his sorrow, his anger.

His parents would never understand. His father might, one day, but Ammi ... she was a hopeless case. Hopelessly out of tune with today's world. Living in the glories of her childhood. Well, never was she going to be a little girl again, nor were those carefree days ever coming back to Kashmir. Unless people like Akram helped to bring them back. Helped to drive out the ubiquitous presence of the uniform. Only then would they all feel safe once again. Only then would they be able to take command of their lives and destinies. Aftab completely believed Akram's truths. There was no room for words such as his mother's.

Aftab wandered on. The sky was leaden and grey. In the distance, the river was thick and slow and reflected the sky. And his mood. It would be many months before the summer forced the river to shake off its lethargy and invite the boys back in to play in its breath-robbing icy waters. Today the sky and river were pensive. Like his mood. The trees, bleak and empty. Like his heart. The side of his right eye throbbed. He gingerly touched it and winced. But it brought a smile of wry satisfaction to his lips. He knew his father would be wracked with guilt when he would see the blue-black bruise. And maybe it would teach his mother to hold her tongue and mind her own business. Maybe she would turn a blind eye for a while.

He felt the bluing bruise on his arm and sighed bitterly. Life was strange. Last night everything had seemed so perfect. Laughing with Akram and Feroze. Now, everything was upside down. His mother was suspicious, his father furious and Amir – stupid. And who knew what went on in Shazia's mind? Worst of all, try as he might, he couldn't dream of the perfect plan. A plan that would make Akram say, 'Wah! hamara Aftab toh sab ka ustaad nikla!' How Javed and Imran would burn with jealousy. Their plans would be rejected. His, Aftab's, would be selected. He would do it. He would carry it out. He would be a hero. The 'anonymous militant' reported in the national dailies. The babus in faraway Delhi would think that they were up against a terrible challenge. There'd be a price on his head. He'd have to run away from home. Away from Ammi and Abbu and their cowardly ways. There, he'd said it, it had to be said, they were cowards who couldn't look at what was staring them in the face. Yes, they would run away from their homes. He and Akram. Akram was the only family he needed – or wanted. They would live in the thickest forest, drinking water from mountain streams, killing game to fill their bellies.

And then, in his mind's eye, the blood flowed – the blood of their kill. Aftab put his hands to his temples to keep his head from swimming at the thought of so much blood. Inadvertently, he pressed the swollen bruise across his eye.

'Ow!' he yelped, shaken out of his glorious reverie. 'Ah, I h-a-t-e him!' he spat out aloud.

'Whom do you hate – me?' drawled a familiar voice. Aftab whirled around and saw, with startled dismay, Akram. Immediately, he was reduced to a stammering idiot. The grey mood melted and the sun came out.

'I – oh – Ak-Akram Bhai, I didn't know … I didn't see.'

'Now, who is it that we hate so much?' Akram slipped an arm around the younger boy's shoulder, 'I hope it's not me, Chottey Bhai?'

'N-no, of course not Akram Bhai, why do you make fun of me. I could never hate you. Never.'

'Thank God for that,' laughed Akram, 'I'd be mortified to be at the receiving end of such wrath.'

'You're really pulling my leg now. You – and frightened? That too of me?'

'A young boy's rage is a frightening thing, believe me. So, you want to tell me about it?' Akram's fingers gently outlined the blackening bruise around his eye. He took in the bruises on his arm, the reddening of the neck. Someone had really dug into the boy. 'Who did this?'

'My father,' it came out in a seething, strangled whisper, 'I hate him.'

'Your father did the right thing!'

'Right thing?' It was like a slap on his face. Worse than any beating his father had ever given him. 'How can you of all people say that, Akram Bhai?' he blurted out.

'He beat you because you were with us last night, isn't it?' Aftab nodded, hanging his head miserably, shamed.

'He is right, you know, these are dangerous games we're playing, in dangerous times.'

'Kya, Akram Bhai, you sound just like my mother.'

The older man threw back his head then, and laughed out aloud. 'Acha, toh ab tum mujhe janani bana rahe ho?'

Only Akram would have had it in him to laugh when compared to a woman, Aftab thought. 'No, no, what I meant ....'

'I know what you mean. But Aftab, don't be angry with your parents. My little brother, they worry for you – and rightly so. Do you know how lucky you are to have parents who love you enough to beat you to protect you? Look at Feroze. He cannot even remember his father's face, the touch of his mother. He longs for them. Yearns for them. More so, because he knows he'll never get them back ever again.'

'Is that why his hands shake so much, Akram Bhai? Um – I hope you don't mind my asking?'

'No, it's alright, your asking. But I want you to keep this to yourself, okay? No gossiping about Feroze in front of the other boys. If I find out you've talked to them I'll have your hide. You'll feel as if your father's beating was a feather's touch.'

'I promise, I swear. You can tell me whatever you like. My lips are sealed.'

'Good. I tell you this only because you'll understand. I know that you're much more sympathetic towards Feroze than those two. I've seen that you've never stared at his trembling, never made fun when he drops something.'

'Akram Bhai, why, I'd never, ever do that.'

'I know it, I've noticed it, but the other two are foolish that way, that's why I wanted to tell you about Feroze, I need someone who knows, someone I know I can depend on to help him when the time comes, you understand?'

Aftab nodded, his heart swelling with pride, he was being chosen because he was sensible, because he could keep a secret. Even though he didn't know what Akram meant when he said, 'When the time comes.' Akram looked into the boy's eyes, seriously assessing him. He liked what he saw – an honesty, an integrity. An unquestioning innocence. An innocence he could use. Now and later. An innocence that was like clay in his hands. He would mould it now ....

Akram started to walk towards the river. Aftab followed. Almost running to keep up with the older man's long strides.

3

Get back home and just deny
everything ...

'Feroze left the mountains that were home and crossed the border with his father and older brother when he was only nine. They left his mother and two sisters behind, promising to send the money back. And to return when the times were better. When they had made lots of money, as they had been promised. Feroze is now twenty-three. He never met his mother or sisters again. Never heard from them either.'

'Not even through letters?'

'The women never learned to read or write. What good would letters be to them?'

'But, someone could have read it out to them.'

'Who? Most of the men were away. Besides, there's no sense in exposing your whereabouts when you're on work like this. It was just safer not to.'

'What about his father and brothers? Are they here in Kashmir as well?'

'No, no. They came to India. But Feroze was taken away from them long before that.'

'Why?' Aftab couldn't imagine being separated from his parents at such a young age, couldn't really imagine life without his mother, in spite of all his fantasies.

'Well, you see how it is with you, your every step is watched by those who worry for you, I know that you have to sneak out to meet us. The father and brothers would always worry about the little one, even if they were a part of it. If he were to be trained properly, he'd have to be on his own. Be a man.'

'B-but he was just a boy, a child ... .'

'There is no time and place for exceptions in this war, haven't you understood that by now?' Akram snapped, truly annoyed. Aftab hung his head and bit his tongue. He had to learn to keep quiet, stop interrupting. Questioning.

'Where was he trained?' he whispered, trying to make amends, ask the right question.

'Across the border. In a camp especially for young boys. They're very good camps. They teach you running, mountain and rock climbing, survival training, high altitude training, making IEDs – improvised explosive devices – and handling all kinds of firepower from pistols to big guns. Guerilla warfare, ambush arms ... really, everything you're likely to need.'

Aftab's imagination was fired. How he longed to be in just such a camp. Rough. Hard. Learning to become a man. Instead here he was, waiting to be served tea in bed by his Ammi. The older man looked askance at the boy and smiled, his words had found their mark. Again.

'Wish you could be trained there too, haan?' Aftab nodded. 'It sounds like fun, I know, but it's really very hard. Some boys, the soft ones, die just in training. Some days you're so tired, your body won't listen to you, but you've got to go on. And on. Because your commander tells you to. On and on.'

'Yeah, but I'm not soft.'

'I know, Aftab, you are no softie. And neither was Feroze.'

'But Feroze didn't. Die, I mean.'

'No, he didn't. In fact, Feroze showed exceptional promise. He had the makings of an A-1 soldier right from the very beginning. He was quick to learn, fearless and had a sharp mind. He was also very agile. He could climb up and down slippery slopes like a mountain goat. Then, when he was just twelve, things began to hot up in India. We lost quite a few good men. It became necessary to fill the vacancies. Normally, a boy this young wouldn't have been sent into the field. But these were not normal times, someone was needed. And Feroze fitted the bill. He was given a mission. He had to sneak into the army camp at night. He had to plant bombs in three different areas of the camp. The plan was a beauty, but of course, it was extremely daring. Dangerous.'

'Then why give it to a twelve-year-old with no previous experience?'

'He was small, you see, so the chance of detection was less. And, like I told you, he was fearless, quick and fast up and down the slopes – important for a quick getaway.'

'And was his mission successful?'

'Oh yes, a beauty. Twenty-seven Indians in uniform were killed. Feroze completed the mission perfectly, except for the last part, the clean getaway.'

'He wasn't caught, was he?'

'He was.' Akram's green eyes darkened with anger as he remembered. Or anguish. Or both.

'They caught him as he reached the bottom of a steep slope. They caught him. They brought him back to the camp and they – they – they brutalized him.'

'What did they do?'

Akram sank down on the rocky bank of the Jhelum. His head hung so low that his chin rested on his chest. He pulled his knees up. It was almost as though he was trying to protect himself from memories too painful to bear.

'What did they do to him?'

'Ah – I – I can't even begin to tell you. It was too awful. They nearly killed him. They broke his bones. They almost bled him to death.'

'B-but he was j-just a boy. A boy my age,' whispered Aftab horrified, trying to imagine the pain, the helplessness, of the boy, the child, alone, cut off from his own, surrounded by enemies. Trying not to imagine the blood.

'He didn't deserve it. Aftab ...,' when Akram looked up, his cheeks were wet with tears. Aftab's eyes brimmed over too. 'He didn't deserve such harsh treatment. They could see he was just a child.'

They sat in silence, each lost in the terrible moments they had just spoken about. Each imagining the fear and pain inflicted on a long-ago child. Then Akram spoke again. In a voice quiet and far away.

'It was war. In a war there are no exceptions. No kindness.'

'Not even to a twelve-year-old child?'

'There was no mercy for Feroze – they would have killed him.'

'But they didn't?'

'That was their weakness – their mistake. They should have ....'

'Killed him?'

'Killed him,' Akram confirmed, to Aftab's amazement.

'How can you say that?'

'We would have killed one of theirs – make no mistake about it. We would have tortured one of theirs, a child if that's who fell in our hands. And then, we would have killed him. Or her. It wouldn't matter. They've created a mortal enemy. It was a child they captured. But it was a wily, dangerous man full of thoughts for revenge who escaped from their clutches that night.'

'So he escaped?' Aftab's voice was weak with relief.

The older man rose up and dusted his phiran, picking out the autumn leaves. He started to walk. Without a word, Aftab followed, for he could see that the story was far from over yet.

Akram continued to tell about the daring raid on the heavily guarded camp where Feroze was held. Akram killed two jawans on duty with a sharp knife to the throat. It made no difference to him. He had killed before. But his heart broke when he lifted Feroze in his arms. Reduced to skin and bone, he was near weightless. He bit down on his own hand to keep from moaning as his fractured limbs were moved. And later, it was revenge, not pain, which burned in his eyes. The determined set of his jaw belied the shaking of his hands. He had become a man and yearned no longer for his mother or sisters, thought no longer of his father and brothers. Now he was married to 'the cause'. And nothing else mattered.

The shaking hands were a constant reminder of that long-ago time. Nicotine helped to still the shattered nerves somewhat, but his mind was always racing, even during the short bursts of sleep that came intermittently through the long, dark nights.

Shaking himself out of a deep reverie, Akram laughed harshly and tousled the boy's hair. 'So you see, Chottey Bhai, your parents know that they must protect you the way only parents can. Never hate them for doing what is their sacred duty.'

'But what about my sacred duty to bring peace to

the valley? What about the sacred duty that I have sworn to you that I will carry out?'

'You must do what you must do. But don't deny your parents' right to do what they must do – right?'

They had reached the bazaar. 'I'm hungry,' said Akram, striding towards the halwai's dhaba. Aftab followed, suddenly realizing how hungry he himself was. The smell of crisp samosas and hot elaichi chai wafted towards him. As they settled down at the table, Aftab noticed the halwai looking over his shoulder at them. He had a look of suspicion in his eye. Then he saw the boy looking at him and hurriedly turned away.

'What's he looking at us for?' murmured Aftab.

'Who?'

'What?'

'What did you say, who's looking at us?'

'No, nothing, I thought the halwai was looking at us funnily.'

Akram ducked his head down between his shoulders. 'Keep an eye on him, if he does anything suspicious, tell me, quick, okay?'

'Okay …,' replied the boy, puzzled and pleased at the same time. Suddenly the dank shop took on the mystery and excitement of a movie set. A song was blaring from an old radio. Everybody seemed to give them suspicious looks. Something was going to happen.

'Can I get you anything, janaab?' Startled, Aftab looked up to see the halwai standing over them, wiping his hands on an already greasy cloth. 'Tea ... just tea,' said Akram. He looked up and stared hard at the halwai. The stare was returned. Both men were challenging each other. Aftab looked from one to the other, wondering what was going on.

'What's going on?' he asked as the halwai left.

'Shh! Let me think.' Akram snapped. Aftab was puzzled. Then he noticed the halwai take a final look at them, whisper something in his young helper's ear and leave the shop.

'He's left the shop ... .'

'What?'

'Lalaji, the halwai, he's left the shop – you, you asked me to tell you if he did anything.'

Akram was on his feet in a flash. 'Quick, get out, get out of here, hurry!' he snapped.

As he hurried to the open doorway, the shopkeeper's helper blocked Akram's path. 'Wait, you haven't had your tea, sir.'

'Here's the money, you drink the tea, with my blessings.'

'Sir, no, wait, don't be in such a hurry, there's special tea being made for you, special.' Lalaji would kill him if he let these two get away.

Akram had the boy by the throat, 'Get out of my way, you snake, you traitor, just get the hell out of my way.' He pushed the boy, who fell backwards onto the tandoor just behind him. He shrieked as hot liquid splashed over him. 'Help, bachao, don't let them get away.'

Pulling Aftab after him, Akram ran out of the shop, darting between handcarts and beggars. It had all been so sudden. Aftab couldn't quite make out what had happened. But something had. The adrenaline rushed through his veins, the blood roared in his ears as he pounded after Akram. He hardly noticed that the other's fingers bit hard into his arm. They were running. Together. Fear and pride. Pride and fear. Running. Together. Both of them.

They reached the woods. Aftab's dreams were coming true. They were on the run together. They were going to hide here, in the woods. Akram seemed to have turned into a wild animal. A part of the forest. He looked around, his eyes darting. Hunting for prey. Or was he the hunted? Aftab stared at him, too out of breath to ask or question. 'Suno, Chottey Bhai, you leave now. Get back home. Go directly home. And just deny everything. Leave.' Akram gave him a little push. Aftab was aghast. This is not how he had planned things should be.

'What about you? I'm not going to leave you like this.'

'There's no time, go – just go … get out now.'

'Why can't I hide here with you? We'll be together.'

'You'll slow me down. I can't have the army and your father on my heels. I said get out, now go.'

'But, how will I meet you? How will I know you're alright?'

'I'll be in touch – get out … .'

And within minutes he was gone, melting into the woods. Magic. Aftab stood there, stunned. Disappointed. The adrenaline plummeted, draining him out. He felt deflated, as if he'd been thrown away like garbage. Then he heard the dogs. He heard voices. He knew he had to get out of there. Otherwise he would lead the enemy to his friend.

And Aftab ran. As fast as he could. His heart wanted to go one way, but his head urged him on in the other. All he knew now was that he had to get away. To safety. Home.

4

He was not alone, sir.

Not alone ...

The halwai ran as fast as his slippers and paunch would allow. Behind him were army jawans, led by Major Ramneeq. The Major was a star athlete and had held a national record for the 1500 m. He fought his every instinct now, not to sprint ahead of the fat halwai. He couldn't bear to run behind the man who was slowing him down. But he knew that his best chance was the element of surprise. Cornering the rogue militant in the shop would be his best bet of catching him. As they approached the shop, however, the halwai's young helper stood outside gesticulating wildly. Something had happened. Something was amiss.

'They left saab, ran away.'

The halwai came puffing up behind Major Ramneeq, 'Idiot!' he panted, and landed a sharp blow on his servant's ear.

'Oh ho, bus, that's enough!' the army man commanded, catching the boy before he fell. 'What happened, tell me. Calmly, slowly.'

But before the boy could speak, the Lala tightened his grip on his helper's arm, obviously cautioning him. He led the party into his shop and ordered tea for all of them. Then he sat down and narrated the entire story, eyes rolling, arms flaying. As if his very life had been in danger. The boy stared sullenly at his employer and touched his back where he'd been scalded. It was he whose life had been threatened by the firangi. It was he whose throat was grabbed, who was flung aside as both the terrorists, or whoever they were, fled. 'It was me, not him ...,' he thought sulkily, but then his thoughts came to an abrupt halt. He listened carefully to what the Lala was saying. What was this? He was leaving out some details.

'Phir saab, I noticed this man – a firangi staring at me with murder in his bloodshot eyes. I could see that his intentions were not good. I think he meant to kidnap me. You know that I am a rich man by local standards. I have noticed this man loitering outside my house. He must have been planning my kidnapping, sir and ....'

'Was he alone?'

The halwai hesitated, then said, 'Alone, saab ... he was alone. Who would keep company with such a rogue?' He looked up and met his helper's shocked eyes. Then he looked back at the army man, 'Yes, sir, he was alone. There was no one with him.'

Major Ramneeq noticed the hesitation. He noticed the exchange of looks between the halwai and his helper. His instinct told him that something was not quite right. 'You're sure he was alone?' he asked again.

'The firangi was alone, sir, you know that we all hate these foreigners who have made our lives a living hell. How many have left their homes. How many of us bed down before it's dark, living in fear of being discovered by these rogues. No sir, no local would have associated with them, sir.'

Again the exchange of looks.

'Look, Lalaji, I have a feeling that you're not quite telling the truth. If there's something more you need to tell us, you should do so. The consequences of lies in such things can be, well, painful.'

'Kya sirji, now you are threatening me, saab. Me, an upright, honest citizen whose been doing his mite to help you, sir.'

'So, your firangi was alone, then?'

'Alone sir, alone, ask anyone. Ask Chottu here, he'll tell you. He saw it all. Kyon Chottu, the firangi terrorist was here on his own, alone, na?'

The boy nodded, head down, unable to meet anyone's eye. What was happening here? he wondered. *Why these half-truths? Who was Lalaji protecting? And why?*

Pretty soon it was over. The tension, the uniformed presence, the excitement of the moment were gone.

'Lalaji?' asked Chottu timidly, 'Why …?'

'Arre Chottu, you did well, beta, keeping your mouth shut.'

'But why didn't you …?'

'Why didn't I what? Betray one of our own families? Tattle on a little boy who plays cricket with my son? Turn in a child whom I've carried on these very shoulders?'

'You know the boy?'

'Of course, arre, his father is a good man. A schoolteacher, his mother, a decent, godfearing woman. He has a younger brother, and a sister all ready for nikaah. Sari family barbaad ho jaati. And what would I have gained, by harming a perfectly decent family?'

'But Lalaji,' protested the boy, 'He was with the foreigner, you saw it with your own eyes, didn't you?'

'You don't worry your simple head over it. I'll, I'll talk to the boy, talk to his father. That's all that's needed, not the army to get after our innocent people. Let them concentrate on the foreign terrorists, that's enough. Now, we've wasted enough time – get back to work.

'Ji, Lalaji, I'll, I'll get the ration – we're low on sugar, salt and tea.'

'But hurry it up, understand – no loitering in the bazaar with your good-for-nothing friends, samjhe?'

'Right, Lalaji, main bus abhi gaya aur abhi aya … .'

Chottu ran. Zigzagging through the carts, shoppers and beggars. His breath grew ragged. Soon, his legs were shaking with exertion, fear and excitement. Chottu reached the contingent of soldiers, as they were about to enter the Cantonment. He rushed up, grabbed Major Ramneeq's arm and blurted out, 'He was not alone, sir, not alone ....'

Aftab ran. Making his way through trees, darting into the safety of shadows. Out of breath, his legs shaking with exertion, fear and excitement. Aftab reached his garden gate. Gasping, he tried to catch his breath to steady himself before he went in and was confronted by his parents. But then he heard the sound of running feet. Sure that someone had caught up with him, he charged into the door and ran straight into the army officer who filled the tiny space with his presence. And his gun.

'Steady, steady boy,' the officer caught him before he keeled right over. 'Steady, catch your breath. Get him a drink of water.' The officer commanded Shazia, Aftab's sister, with a look. Anger welled up in the boy, mingling with fear, making him nauseous.

Who is he, this, this uniformed stranger, to order Aapa around like a maid? Aftab squirmed out of the man's grasp and strode purposefully to the kitchen. He was quite capable of fetching water for himself.

'Why are they looking for you?' Shazia hissed, holding out the glass to him.

'How do I know?' Aftab's fingers closed around the glass, but his sister did not relinquish it right away.

'Don't be a fool, have you got an answer to give him?'

'What? I … I … what answer? I don't have to give him an answer.'

'Idiot! Never use your brain, do you?' hissed Shazia angrily, 'Now listen to me, carefully. When he asks where you've been, say that the man had taken you by force.'

'Never!'

'Shut up and listen. There's no time — say that he threatened to abduct me if you didn't give him money. You'd gone to negotiate the amount with him.'

Abruptly, Shazia let go of the glass and some water splashed onto both of them. Her green eyes glittered a warning as she turned away.

'Kya khus phus kar rahe ho, tum dono?' Abbu was behind Aftab, leading him back to where the army man stood, smelling of leather and guns. Aftab's mind reeled. What did Shazia mean? He would never let Akram down. Never. His ears burned with shame, just at the thought of accusing his beloved leader of an act so lowly and vile as the abduction of his sister. Why, he'd rather die. Yes, yes, he would undergo any beating his father meted out, any torture the army subjected him to, before he would accuse Akram to save his skin. Yes, they would have to cut his tongue off before it would wag against his mentor. Yes.

'Hurry up, don't keep Major saab waiting. And remember, there's nothing to be afraid of — just tell the truth — the simple truth.' Abbu's voice was high and jovial — loud. As if he was at a social gathering. 'Come son, don't be shy. Major saab wants to ask you some questions that you must answer honestly.

Yes, honestly, after all, there's nothing you have to hide, hai na? Major saab, I think our little ranjha has some aashique tucked away somewhere. Kyon Romeo – off to meet your girlfriend, were you?' And here, the father held the boy's bony shoulder tightly. A warning – a suggestion?

'So, Aftab – that is your name, is it not?' the army man lifted the boy's chin, forcing him to look up into his eyes.

'Yes, sir.'

'And where have you been, Aftab – not up to any mischief, I hope?'

'N-no, sir, no.'

'So, where have you been?'

'Nowhere, sir, just …. 'Aftab's voice trailed off.

From the corner of his eye, he met his sister's glaring, green stare, urging him to do better. He knew he'd better have something more substantial to say, but he wondered: how much the officer knew? And he would never follow Aapa's instructions and frame Akram. Never. But chee, he'd never say that he was involved with some girl either; besides, then they'd want to know her name, house, want to question her, maybe. And then what?

Major Ramneeq's fingers tightened around his chin as he jerked his head up – imperceptibly. But firmly.

'The truth now, boy. Why were you so out of breath – so frightened? What were you running from? I want the truth.'

41

The officer's fingers were hard. His eyes closely examined the bruises on the boy's face. The fingers of his free hand explored them questioningly. There were a lot of pieces to this jigsaw puzzle. The Lala's lies – what was he covering up? The boy's hedging, the father's false joviality, the whispering sister, the mother who wouldn't meet his gaze. Who had beaten the boy. And why?

'The truth,' Major Ramneeq barked as the vision of the brutalized bodies of the boys killed from his division reared up.

'The truth, boy, the truth. I want to know the truth – and I'll have the truth.'

5

Hang your head in shame, boy,
what have you done?

'He forced me,' the words spilled out as easily as the tears from his eyes.

'He – who?'

'The f-firangi,' Aftab shuddered with self-hate at what he was doing, at the hated word that he used now to describe his mentor. 'The firangi,' he sobbed. He heard Shazia let out the breath she'd been holding. The Major lifted the boy's face to look into his eyes.

'He forced you? But you were sitting and drinking tea with him. You didn't look like you were forced. You were having a good time, talking, smiling.'

The accusing finger was pointing right at Aftab, making him cross-eyed with fear. 'I was ne-ne-negotiating, trying to make a deal ....'

'Deal? You filthy pup, what do you think you're doing, making deals with our enemies?' It was the father, this time, whose voice pounded in Aftab's ears and heart as he was spun around. He rubbed his chin, feeling bruised, burned where the officer's fingers had been.

Major Ramneeq held the father back, grasping the raised hand before it landed on the boy and spoilt it all. The Major had more subtle tools of interrogation and he would not let an irate father wreck it.

'Please step back, step away,' he commanded. 'I request you all to leave the room please. I would like to talk to the boy alone for some time.' And here, just a subtle pressure on the boy's back. A subtle warning of things to come. A satisfying shudder shot through the boy. The Major nodded. This wouldn't take long. The boy wouldn't need much persuasion.

'He's a good boy, Major saab, he hasn't done anything, he ... .' The Major held up a hand to silence the mother, whose voice was raised to a hysterical pitch.

'I know he's a good boy, the best. And I know he's an honest boy too, who'll tell the truth. He has nothing to hide. Now please ... .' As the family left, the army man turned his attention squarely to the boy. He held him by his shoulders.

'Now look at me boy, look me in the eye and tell me the entire story. And I want no lies, you hear? Lies make me angry, very, very angry.' He tightened his grip to emphasize his words.

The image of Feroze's shaking hands, Akram's descriptions of his broken body clutching at his heart, Aftab fabricated the best lies that had ever rolled off his tongue.

'I was down by the river.'

'Alone?'

'Yes.'

'Why alone?'

'Because because I'd had a quarrel with Abbu-Ammi, then my friends wouldn't let me bat first ....'

The shadow of a smile lit up the older man's eyes, but he quelled the sudden wave of tenderness from his heart. This was a suspect. Not his son. 'So, you were angry?'

'Yes.'

'Then?'

'So, I sat by the river, skipping stones – or trying to – I'm not very good at skipping stones.'

'Go on.' Aftab saw the hint of the smile again.

'I heard someone behind me. It was, it was the ....' The word caught at his throat.

'The firangi?'

'Y-yes.' *Traitor*, said his heart.

'Go on,' the officer said.

Silence.

'Had you seen him before?'

'No, never.' *Liar liar*.

'Do you have a name for him?'

'He never said – I – I didn't ask.' *Akram Bhai, Akram Bhai, I'm sorry.*

'These bruises on your face – did he hit you?'

'Yes, yes, he thrashed me.' *Miserable gaddaar, hang your head in shame boy, what have you done?* 'H-have you caught him, sir?'

'No, no the swine gave us the slip.'

Thank God – relief. The Major saw the look. Relief? Surely not. Fear – surely, surely?

'What did he say, go on …,' gentler now.

Slowly, inexorably, the lies were spun.

'He called me by my name. Said he had been watching me.'

'Why you?'

'Because – because of Aapa.' *Traitor.*

'Your sister?'

'Yes, he said, he said he'd been watching Shazia Aapa – he said that she's very beautiful. He said, he said … .' *Yellow-livered coward.* 'I had to get hold of money to save my sister. I begged him to lessen the amount. Where would I get a thousand rupees from? But … .'

Major Ramneeq was silent. The pieces of the jigsaw were falling into place. Weren't they? He squinted into the boy's eyes, looking for guile and deceit. But he found tears instead. Tears that made the bile rise in the older man's throat. These militants. They'd stop at nothing to get their way. Threaten a little boy with his sister's izzat! The sister, yes.

She was achingly beautiful, heartbreakingly innocent. An easy target. Where would they go next? How low would they stoop?

He looked into the boy's clear eyes. Could he trust him, take him at his word? Whom did the tears in those eyes glisten for? Well, truth or lies, the boy was a lead. And Major Ramneeq was not about to give up a lead so precious. He would appoint a couple of his jawans to tail the boy, watch his comings and goings discreetly. If the boy told the truth, then the foreign mercenary would try to contact him to collect his 'protection' money. And if the boy had lied and was protecting the militant, well, that would come out too. But the Major hoped that it wouldn't come to that. He liked this young lad. He knew it couldn't be helped. And yet.

The bile rose in the boy's throat too. He hated his tongue for the lies it had wagged. He was heartsick with the things he had been forced to say. But if he hadn't, there would have been blood. Blood. His blood everywhere. The dying shrieks of the long ago sacrificial lamb mingled with the shrieks that must have rent the air, when Feroze was being tortured. Shrieks throbbed through Aftab's brain. Then he could taste blood. His blood.

The boy had bitten through his lying tongue and blood spurted out of his mouth. The metallic smell of the blood made him dizzy and once again the Major had to support him to stop him from keeling over.

Then it was over. The Major was gone. The boy was comforted by his mother. He met his sister's wry smile once, but then looked away, too ashamed.

'You did right, you did right, son,' said Abbu, finally proud of his son. If only he knew. *If only he knew.* His mother soothed him, pouring apologies into his burning ears, 'I'm sorry, mere lal, if only I knew, I would never have scolded you. And Abbu, Abbu would have helped you, not hit you. Forgive me, son, forgive me.' The tears that came then, rolling down her cheeks onto his own, were too much. The guilt and shame were choking him. He needed air. Fresh air. Abruptly, he left the room and slammed the door shut behind him.

He stood, gulping in the chilled air, and closed his eyes. Trying to put the day's events in order. Trying, trying to think ahead. Was he now an outcast? After squealing on his beloved Akram Bhai, was he ever going to be part of the inner circle again? His imagination led him to an illusionary meeting. Without him. Akram telling Javed and Imran about Aftab's fateful treachery. Warning them against ever meeting him again. 'Aftab,' said Akram with hate in his voice as he spat into the corner – the very name too vile, too unclean to be taken again. *Shameshameshameshame.*

'You did well,' startled back to reality, Aftab met Shazia's smile. 'Good boy, you did well to do as you were told,' she repeated.

'What? What do you mean – I told the truth – nothing more, nothing less.'

'Ah yes,' Shazia laughed out loud, 'The truth – amazing how truthful you sounded, no? I could hear you through the door. We were all listening. It was a good touch, by the way, to bite your tongue to distract the good Major saab and stop the questions. A good touch – well done, you're a big hero now, at home. Saving your sister from evil men – good little, good little boy,' she patted his curly head. A touch of sisterly indulgence. A touch of sarcasm.

'It wasn't a trick – a touch. I was telling the truth. He, the firangi, did threaten me that he'd abduct you if I didn't cough up the money. It's the truth.'

Suddenly the hand on his head was no longer sisterly. She grabbed his short-cropped curls and yanked his head back so he'd have to look her in the face.

'Now don't be a fool, Aftab. If you're such a fool, you better not play these war games.'

'OW!' he pulled away, then turned on her, his guilt and shame turning to anger now. 'Games, games, games – why do all of you, ALL of you call them games? They're not games – they're not. It is serious business. We're fighting for freedom – your freedom. Don't you understand that?'

'Dekho, little Boey, I understand a lot of this business – maybe even a bit more than you ....'

'Ha!'

'Yes, ha! Go ahead, go ahead and laugh. Just because I'm a girl, it doesn't mean that I don't know things that you've probably never even dreamed about. I use my brains and, if you're going to keep that silly hide of yours in one piece, you'd better learn to do the same too, samjhe?'

'Oh ho, the great woman freedom fighter is ... .'

'Shazia, oh Shazia, kuri, stop your khusar pusar and help me pick the rice clean. Really, you're all ready to be married, but you still behave like a child.'

'Coming, Ammi.'

'So, what is it that you've thought about with that fancy brain of yours?' persisted Aftab, pleased, now that his sister had been summoned to the kitchen, where she did, after all, belong.

'Well — it's not over with the Major, is it?' she turned to her brother.

'Of course, he was convinced with my story — there's nothing more for him to ask.'

'Fool!' she barked, 'The army's not stupid, you know. He's got a lead, don't you see? You're his lead. He's going to be back. He's going to ask you a lot of questions. Mark my words, they're going to keep an eye on you, they're going to try to recruit you to help them catch the militant,' she concluded, pleased with herself now, looking at her brother's paling face. It was obvious that he hadn't thought of any of this. Hadn't used his brains. As usual. But when she looked out of the window a little while later, she couldn't help smiling at the sight of her little Boey starting his stretching exercise. He'd be busy for an hour at least now. He'd become obsessive about his bodybuilding. That was good. It would keep him out of trouble. At least for a little while.

That night, Aftab's head reeled with a hundred thoughts. It had been a long, long day that had started off badly and only gotten worse. He lay awake, too tired, too anxious to sleep. The candles burned low. The electricity had gone again, but Abbu was up reading. The zing and ping of moths and beetles crashing into the windowpanes outside only added to the boy's restlessness. He felt rather like those beetles – smashing himself blindly towards the light that was Akram and his mission. Like those idiotic beetles, he too failed miserably. Succeeding only in battering himself. Nothing more. Shazia was right. She would use her brain. She would get in, using her brains. He, on the other hand, would lie, bashed and bruised. Outside. Useless.

'No,' he told himself, 'I will not be useless. I will learn to use my head. I'll learn from Aapa. From Akram Bhai, from Feroze. I will do something. I'll prove myself.'

As his mind ticked, it suddenly occurred to him. Someone had betrayed him. Someone who had known him had named him to the Major. Who could it be? Who hated him enough to want the army on his tail? Who?

Lalaji? Aftab's blood ran cold. It had to be Lalaji. Who else? Lalaji, who had come to the hospital with laddoos when Amir was born. Aftab he still remembered how Lalaji had placed him high on his shoulders after popping a warm, fresh laddoo in his mouth and taken him to the hospital nursery where the babies were kept. How Lalaji had pointed out one pink blob lying amongst others and said, 'Yehi hai tumahara chotta bhai, you are a big brother now, a big, big boy.'

The pride then. The horror now. Would Lalaji have to pay the price for his deceit?

Aftab closed his eyes to images of what could happen to Lalaji. Instead, he tried to imagine where Akram was. What was he up to? He would seek him out tomorrow. He would explain what had happened with Major saab, he would beg Bhai's forgiveness for telling filthy lies about him. He would try to make amends. He would tell him about Lalaji's betrayal. Perhaps Akram Bhai would allow him to take revenge on Lalaji. Then he would have proved himself.

By the light of the sputtering candles, Aftab's eyes travelled up to the tiny hole in the wire netting stretched across the window by his bed. A little beetle, no bigger than the nail on his little finger, was squeezing its way through the hole. And then it was in. It had found a way, while the others still battered themselves against the glass and wire mesh impotently.

Aftab's eyes followed the progress of the beetle as it shook itself, once in. It paused for a moment, taking stock of the situation. Then flew straight towards the light and immolated itself on the flame.

Aftab smiled. Yes. He too would stop battering

against glass. He too would find that hole in the wire netting. He too would make it inside.

And then, he too would immolate himself on the flame that was Akram Bhai's mission.

As his father finally blew out what remained of the candles, Aftab turned over, satisfied. He would find a way. He would.

And then, finally, he slept.

6

He felt no guilt at the deaths that had
occurred at his hand

Akram lay panting in his secret lair. It was a hollow
cave, deserted by a leopard or a bear. It still had the
secret smell of a secretive animal. Held close to its heart.
And this, Akram knew, was to his advantage. The dogs, if
the forces put them after him, would be confused by the
animal scent that masked the cave. And then, just to be on
the safer side, Akram had taken the long way, through the
river. Wading through its icy embrace for a good mile
or so.

Now he lay panting, trying to catch his breath.
Trying to still the shake in his legs trembling with
exertion and chill. Maybe some fear, although that he
would never admit, even to himself.

As soon as he was able to, he stripped off his sopping
wet clothes and made his way deeper into the dark

recesses of his hideout to where he had stashed away a couple of sets of warm, dry clothes. Bliss! Moving to another overhanging ledge, he stretched up and pulled down a hurricane lamp, matches, tea leaves, sugar and dry bakarkhani. He was grateful for this forethought — stocking up for just such a day.

Clean and dry now, sipping the thick, sweet tea, Akram took stock of his situation. He knew he was safe here. No one knew of the hideout. No, not even Feroze. This was his secret. His alone.

Unfortunately, he had been seen by many in the bazaar in the company of Aftab. He himself had been anonymous so far, but now he was identifiable through Aftab. Aftab was a local boy. Therefore, Aftab was traceable. For the first time, the boy would be put to the test. Would he be able to withstand the sight or even the thought of blood? Ah yes, Akram knew of the child's pathological fear of blood. He hadn't yet let on that he knew. He was keeping that little piece of information for a time when he could use it. Just in case some blade needed strategic twisting. But if the army drew blood, would he squeal? Would he lead them to him? No, he knew nothing about this hideaway. But would he be strong enough to withstand the inevitable questioning and not give away details of their little group? Yes, yes, he was a good boy. Not too strong, but loyal, desperate for his, Akram's, approval. Akram had grown quite fond of him. And he knew that the boy hero-worshipped him.

Akram smiled as he remembered the boy's eyes shining in adoration. No, he would not let him down. Yet, was he strong enough to withstand the questioning by the army? Smart and quick-witted enough to throw them off his track? That he wasn't sure about.

Then it occurred to Akram. Aftab was sure to try to seek him out. To find out if he was alright. Safe. But the army was going to keep an eye on the boy. He was their lead and they would try to get him to lead them to his lair. Either overtly, or, if Aftab didn't give in, covertly. Akram knew now that he would have to hide, not only from the army, but also from his very own follower. It would hurt the boy, it would fill him with frustrated anxiety, but there was no choice. He'd have to depend on the others to bring him some supplies. He'd have to lie low a while.

Tonight, he decided, he would have to stay indoors. Tonight he would have to make do with this bare fare of tea and dry bread. It was too dangerous to venture out. He would gather his thoughts. He would think of a plan. Tonight, he would only think.

And, although he tried to marshal his thoughts, his mind kept going back to the heavenly scents of frying samosas and dripping, syrupy jalebis. The ones left untouched, uneaten in the halwai's shop. Akram sighed. It irritated him when he couldn't control his thoughts. He pulled out the rolled up blanket from the ledge where he kept his supplies. Wrinkling his nose at the musty odour, he forced himself to lie down on the hard floor. Then he pried his mind away from the thoughts of hot food to the longagotime when he was just a little, insignificant fish in a big, big pond ....

As he closes his eyes on the exertions of the day, Akram is transported, back to his days with the big militant outfit. The one reported, written about in every newspaper across the state, the country and indeed, the world, sometimes. The one whose leaders' faces stare down in caricature from the walls of post offices and police stations.

Akram is young. His only claim to fame is when he took part in the operation to rescue Feroze. 'Shabash', one of his leaders says, 'Shabash', along with a little congratulatory pat on the shoulder, before he turns away to ponder over bigger, more pressing issues. Young Akram watches television non-stop, but, though the total number of security men dead that day include the two he had killed, nothing more is said about his part in the daring rescue from the heart of the army camp. He scans the newspaper. Nothing. Not even a mention. Akram is still just an also-ran, fetching and carrying tea and newspapers for the group's big bosses. In spite of all that he has done, in spite of the blood he has spilled with his own hands, the voices, screams he has cut off forever, even today, he can walk unnoticed through the streets and markets merely buying vegetables and salt. He is not wanted. Not by the security forces. Not by his own group. He's an errand boy.

No militant. In spite of everything. In spite of all his effort.

Young Akram chafes at the bit like a fettered horse. He is getting impatient. But no one notices the boy's broadening shoulders, the sprouting beard, the growing restlessness. Not until ….

Akram sits up, unable to deal with the memories again. Yet again. But they couldn't be shelved now. They aren't stopping. Although he stands moodily, looking out at the deepening twilight at the mouth of his hideout, the memories come swarming back like the black clouds of ravens winging noisily homewards.

… Young Akram is being sent to the godown across the Wullar Lake. To where an underground hideout is used to stockpile ammunition. Akram is to touch bullets, gun oil, grease. Akram is not supposed to pick up the wire, gun powder, batteries and other stuff. But Akram recognizes these as the ingredients to make an IED. And he slips these things into his phiran. No one needs to know. One day, he may need this stuff.

His secret burns holes in his pocket, into his wild imagination. It feeds into his restlessness. His fingers itch to put the thing together and blow up – oh – anything – anyone with it. It is time for action and the impetuous youth can wait no longer. And he doesn't.

'Explosion in crowded bazaar', scream the headlines.

'Militant outfits condemn the death of many innocents'.

'No group will own up to the heinous act'.

And more. Much more.

A stinging slap across the face. Then a bunched fist hits him on his mouth, leaving a chipped tooth and a broken nose. And the taste of blood.

The young boy is stunned, reeling. But worse, much worse, he is being humiliated. He is stood in the middle of the smoke-darkened room and he is being. Hit. Hurt. Humiliated.

Long after the. Sting of a slap. Sings the sting of shame.

Bewakoof! Blithering idiot!

Who gave you the authority?

To blow up civilians

People

We've lost peoples'

Faith

Trust

Sympathy

Coward! You've killed women and children

Women and children

Coward!

The words whip worse than the hands. Eyes that ignored him earlier are focussed on him now. Full of anger. Hate.

In spite of himself. In spite of all the time that has inexorably rolled by since that day, Akram's moss-green eyes still fill with tears of remembered shame as he grasps the green moss that overhangs the cave's entrance. Will the pain and humiliation never go away? Will the word 'coward' always follow him like an evil shadow shackled to his every move? But he is NOT a coward; he knows that, surely everyone knows that. His action was not the action of a coward.

It was then that he decided that he'd not be a small fish any more. In the stealth of night, Akram, the boy, gathered up his few belor ings and stole away. Never to come back to the big bosses who took no notice of the grass that grew, strong and wild, beneath their very feet.

Not knowing where he was going, aware of the curfew that he was breaking. Akram spent the first of many nights in the hush of the forest. The song of the crickets, the rumble of the mountain stream kept the lonely boy company and comforted him through that long first night. Worse, much worse than the first night he'd spent away from his home, his mother knowing that he was unlikely to return to that warm, safe haven ever again. He had come away out of boredom, out of a restless spirit, lured like a fish spying a bright bait. Bobbing. And he'd been hooked after that. Forever. He was a long way away from that now, now that he'd lost his second home. But this time there was no bright bait to snare, only the dark clouds of humiliation. The stamp of a 'coward' painted his future.

Life was not easy for him. Hunted, as he was, both

by the security forces and his own militant outfit who knew that he knew too much, he learned to live invisibly. Snatching food whenever he could. Becoming one with the trees and brown earth. Bleaching himself into the snow that came eventually. Then, mingling into the green of the trees in the summer. And in his chest, his heart hardened. He felt no guilt at the deaths that had occurred at his hands. Not even of the women and children. What was all the fuss about anyway? It wasn't as if it was the first time that women and children had died. It was part and parcel of the freedom struggle they were involved in. People died everyday. What was the need to have made such a show? What was the need to humiliate him like that? One of their own? No one would ever do that to him again, he vowed. He would make his mark. He would show the world that Akram Raza was a force to reckon with. Eternity would know him. Would recognize him. Would know what he had done. They might admire him or revile him. But never, never again would they ignore him, humiliate him. Again.

And out of the hurt, the humiliation, the wounded pride, was born the Kashmir Azadi Group, or KAG. It had no members, at first, but it had a leader – young, dynamic, determined. Ruthless. Rootless. A leader who owed allegiance to none but himself. And to prove himself, he would do anything. Anything.

Feroze was his first recruit. It was Feroze who had hunted him out. And succeeded in doing so where others had failed. He had come up, quietly, quietly

behind Akram, as he crouched, gathering mushrooms
that pushed their fresh heads out of the wet earth.
Quietly. But not quietly enough. For Akram was upon
him, swarming all over him. Knee in chest, fingers
gripped around throat. Flat on his back, Feroze, taken
completely by surprise, gasped, 'Akram, Akram Bhai – its
me, me. Have you forgotten your shagirdh – your faithful
follower?'

'I have no followers,' growled the other, 'I am
alone.'

'You're alone no more, Akram Bhai. I am with you.
How can I ever forget how you rescued me? I owe my life
to you. You are my life. My life is yours. How then did
you expect me to stay on with them, with them?' He spat
then, displaying his disgust for those who had mistreated
the man to whom he owed his life.

Akram looked at his first recruit with a mixture of
pride and disdain. Pride, for, yes, he indeed was a
loyalist whose very life he had saved with such daring.
Disdain, dismay, almost, for, as he observed the
shaking hands, the wild, wide look in smoke-grey eyes,
Akram feared that he may be more of a hindrance than
a help.

Feroze followed the gaze. He saw the shaking limbs
had been noted. He saw that the look was not one of
confidence. Far from it. 'These hands,' he began, holding
them out to show that he was not one to wish away a
weakness, 'These hands that shake are not the total of
Feroze bin Ismail. There are things in here and here,' he

said, indicating his head and heart, 'That will be worthy of your trust and leadership. I will never allow these legs to slow you down. Only say that I can join you, for I will never go back to those who do not recognize the treasure that shines beneath their very noses.'

Akram couldn't conceal the smile on hearing this, 'How long have you been preparing this speech?'

And both men laughed. Relieved to have each other. If no one else.

7

Aftab's mind was a storm of
troubled thought

After a restless night, Aftab finally awoke to a cold, grey, mist-enclosed dawn. Bleak. He went through the motions of the morning in a withdrawn daze. His parents, sensing his mood, left him largely to himself. Finally, breakfast, bath and tidying done, Aftab took permission to leave the house. After a word of caution from both the anxious parents, Aftab was slipping his arms into his commodious phiran and slipping out into the mist. He hadn't even reached the gate, however when he heard Amir, his little brother, behind him.

'Bhai,' Aftab stopped. He hated being stopped for last minute instructions. Must be Ammi telling me to be careful, he thought.

'Bhai, wait, wait for me.' Amir caught up with him, heels pressing down on half worn shoes, phiran askew, half on, half off.

'Where'd you think you're off to?' growled Aftab.

'Bhai, I'll come with you today. See, I'm ready. Aaj mein aapke saath hee jaooga.'

'Bewakoof! Who sent you? Whose put you up to this – Ammi?'

'No, no one, Aftab Bhaiya, I – I just wanted to be with you, that's all …,' he trailed off, his brown eyes dripping with appeal, brown, tousled locks falling in front of them. 'Please, Bhai, let me come with you today?'

'I've no time, I've got things to do, important things. Things you won't understand. Go away, leave me alone.' With that, the older brother turned on his heel and strode away, but the younger boy was not one to be shaken off so easily.

'Please Bhai, I'll be quiet, I'll do as you say, I won't trouble you. You, you won't even know I'm there. Please Bhai ….'

Suddenly Amir was on the grassy verge. 'I said, leave me alone. Get off my back. Get out and go make friends of your own,' shouted Aftab, pushing his brother aside. Abruptly, he turned away, not wanting to see the hurt in those eyes, the wobbly chin, who knows, even the tears and runny nose that must follow.

Resolutely, without looking back, Aftab set off down the street. He couldn't possibly take little Amir with him today, he reasoned with himself. He had to find Akram, explain what happened. It could be dangerous, no place for a little kid like his baby brother.

It helped ease the guilt a little. He was doing it for his little brother's protection, after all.

Unknown to the two brothers, hidden eyes had watched their altercation. When the older one strode away, two scruffy gujjars high up on the grassy verge moved too. One whistled to the brown and black gaddi dog that followed obediently behind them. They began to move down, towards the road, headed the same way as the boy who walked purposefully towards an unknown destination.

Aftab's mind was a storm of troubled thoughts. He tried to picture what would happen when he found Akram and the others. It was still early for the meeting, but Feroze was often there early, preparing. Sometimes, Akram would be there with him, discussing things before the younger boys came in. Aftab hoped that that's how it would be today. He needed a little time alone with the men, before the boys came with their snide remarks and jokes. Aftab rehearsed what he was going to say. As he approached the ramshackle hut that served as their meeting place, Aftab dragged his feet. Now that the moment was upon him, he felt he wasn't ready. How could he ever, ever explain the reasons for his betrayal? He should have come clean and told Shazia Aapa everything. Maybe she would have been able to tell him what to say. She was clever with words. With ways of putting things across. Dazzling, even.

No, no, enough with words. Akram Bhai was too, too clever. He would know that the words were someone else's, not Aftab's. He would unravel the web of words and then get to the heart of the truth. And then that would make Aftab look even worse. Not only a traitor, but a liar as well. No, no. Better to be straight. Tell the story like it really was.

Finally, the moment could be put off no longer. With the usual look around, as they had been taught, Aftab assessed whether it was safe to go in. Nothing unusual. Just some kids playing, some shoppers out for vegetables and milk, a couple of old shepherds with their brown dog. Nothing to be suspicious of. It was quite safe. There was no one following him. The boy went in.

The two gujjars stopped and exchanged a brief look. One casually patted the dog's head and pushed him towards the gate of the hut. And then joined the other who sat on the side of the road, lighting up a beedi. The dog ambled over to the gate and sniffed, testing the air. Then he walked towards the door, watched keenly by the gujjars.

The hut was empty. Bereft of any sign of life or habitation. Aftab stood in the middle of the room, dumbfounded. The familiar room looked so unfamiliar now, changed beyond recognition. Moving to a window, Aftab opened it and let in the milky misty enveloping light from outside. But this made things more confusing. For the bare room was filled with the dust and dirt of centuries. Where was the table, the two chairs, the stools, durries that had been such an integral part of the room? Where were the cigarette butts, the matches left by Feroze? Where was the smell of cigarette smoke that clung to the room? Here was only the smell of decay and age and abandonment. Smells that he had never associated with this place that was always abuzz with plans and energy and action. He walked to the corner of the next room. But more dust greeted him instead of the kerosene stove and tea things. Everything, everything was gone. Gone. Long ago. It was as if he had woken up from a long, long sleep and everything in this house had been a dream from another life. The dust motes danced and seemed to mock him, reminding him that they were at home here, not him. Never had been? A strange sensation filled him, was he at the wrong house? Had he somehow lost his way and come into a similar house, by some strange mistake? Lost the way, the way he knew so well he could walk it in his sleep, had often walked it in his dreams?

Helplessly, the boy wandered back to the main room where his lonely footprints in the dust were the only signs of life. Where could he begin to look for his leader now? Why were the others in the group not here? Had they been informed that this place was to be closed down? Did they know where the meeting was to be held instead? And he didn't? He didn't.

Disconsolate, the boy came out into the grey light of day. He loathed to leave just yet. He had nowhere else to go, really. A brown dog greeted him at the door, wagging his huge, plumed tail. In spite of himself, the boy smiled and the dog smiled back at him. The boy patted the massive head, then sank on the front step of the hut. The dog sat with him. Patiently, sniffing at the boy's neck, his hands, his clothes.

The shepherds watched quietly, seemingly engaged in their beedis and talk. They saw their dog familiarize himself with the smell of his quarry. And they were pleased. Things were going well.

As the boy finally left the safe familiarity of the hut and came out, he was joined by the owners of the dog. 'Salaam wallekum, Chottey Mia,' greeted one of the gujjars.

'Walehkum salaam,' the boy returned the greeting, 'Your dog?'

'Hain, yeh Sheru hai, hope he didn't trouble you?'

'Oh no, he's a good dog.' They laughed.

'So, what are you doing, little one, coming out of the old haunted house – you're not a bhut pret yourself are you?'

'Oh no, I'm a flesh and blood boy!' Aftab laughed, glad to have some company after the lonely desolation of the house.

'Well, if you're no ghost, you oughtn't be going in there, it's haunted, they say, haven't you heard?'

'Yes, what made you go in there, anyway?'

'It – I – er – some friends, we, er – we'd decided to meet here, th-that's all,' Aftab wished desperately that Shazia was here. She'd have been able to spin a better yarn than that.

'Hmm, well, tell your friends to find better places to play games, these old houses can be dangerous.'

Games. Games again, thought Aftab disgusted, what did these stupid dim-witted villagers know anyway?

'So, your friends are late are they?'

'Who?'

'Your friends – you had come to meet?'

'Er – y-yes, late, huh! As usual. Well, I'm not going to wait any longer, I'm off, Khuda hafiz.' And abruptly the boy turned to go.

He looked everywhere. Everywhere. But no one from his group was anywhere. Some of the old meeting places, places where they'd hang around, thought Aftab. No one. Not anywhere. It was as if they'd disappeared. Together. Leaving him out. Aftab was heartbroken. How could he ever explain to Akram that he'd had to lie? There wasn't anything else he could do. To protect his family. Himself. Why, even Akram. And the others. He'd lied for them. But where should he begin to look? To find Akram. To explain?

8

Let the boys do the fighting now.
Let the boys do it

Deep in his lair, Akram moved, stretching his cold-stiffened limbs, forcing the pain, the cold, the lethargy to leave him. The day stretched ahead of him. He had to make plans, take decisions. Now that he was on his own, he could take off the carefully crafted mask. It was a relief not to be the leader, not to be the man who was so admired by his little army. So depended upon. For now, he could strip himself of all that burden and be Akram, who had fought his own battles. For himself. But now a great weariness engulfed him in his private moments. He didn't want to fight his own battles. Not really. He wanted someone else to do the fighting for him. To be out there where the action was. Where the danger was. He was through with that. *Let the boys do the fighting now. Let the boys do it.*

At the mouth of the cave, cold hands wrapped around a steaming cup of tea, the green eyes considered the surroundings. And his options. It seemed to him that he was travelling backwards at great speed. Back to the days, when, as a disgraced youngster, he was on his own. Living an animal's invisible life. Akram sighed. He couldn't bear the thought of starting all over again. He didn't have the strength. Or the resolve.

A hangul cried out. A husky scream emerging from the morning mist. Akram shook off his despondent thoughts. He wasn't at square one. He had his team. A good team. It was just a question of strategy and re-grouping. Then, he'd strike and his name would be known. And those who had spat on him in disgust would remember. In awe. And regret. They would think, 'If only he was a part of our team. Or I a part of his.' They would remember him from the newspaper reports. Ah yes, Akram stepping out of his secret home was strong again. Sly, strong, stealthy.

He would teach a bitter lesson to those who had thrown him out like a dog. They were jealous. Yes, that was it. They were jealous of his courage. His daring. His speed and agility. His looks. He was better than them in every way. His arrogance worn like a cloak of honour. But they were the big names. The big league. Well, he'd be there soon. He would. Something so audacious, so startling would happen. People would wonder who could have done it? Especially those who would be suspected, but would know it wasn't them. Couldn't be them, for they'd never dare what he would. And when they would get to know, they would regret. Oh yes, they'd regret that he was no longer part of them. That they'd never be part of him. Yes, he would. No matter what the cost. No matter how many lives it took — lives of women and children. He didn't care. Their bodies would be his stepping stones.

Out of the corner of his ever-watchful eye, he saw a bush startle with movement. Stealthily, he put the chipped cup down onto a waiting rock. Eyes narrowing on a trembling leaf, he crept on cat's feet, forward. The hunger in his stomach as keen as the hunger in his heart. Which yearned to feel the thrill of life ebbing out of a once live thing. Once Akram had the predator awake and hungry in him, there was little chance for the being he had set his sights on. Be it animal, or bird. Or human.

It was like taking a drug. It made him feel exhilarated, got his blood pumping. Made his adrenaline shoot up. It was one of the major problems he had had with his old group. 'You kill because you have to — because you must.' They'd said.

'I kill because I love it!' he'd smiled up at Sajid, his old boss. He'd killed a wild boar. Of course, he couldn't eat the filthy pig. But it had been snorting so stupidly. Just asking for its neck to be broken. And he, Akram, had obliged and laughed with glee as the snorts turned to squeals to screams to nothingness as the life fluid ebbed from the rotten creature. It had sent Sajid into one of his huge rages. But, like a drug addict, Akram had been too doped by the thrill, too exhilarated to be even touched by the ranting. He loved the kill and if someone had a problem with that, it was their problem, not his. He had killed and he would do it again. And again. Because it excited him. Because he loved it.

A scream, a whimper. A little thrashing. And it was over. The black jungle fowl's dying eye stared in shock at its killer. The eyes glittered back with pleasure – oh this was fun. Albeit too brief to be truly satisfying. But it had quenched one hunger. And now he lit up a fire and began to pluck the sodden feathers to quench the other.

His thoughts strayed again to Aftab. He was a good boy. He would listen to every command he, Akram, gave him. Akram knew that the boy hero-worshipped him completely, unquestioningly. Was in love with him, like a girl. Almost. He was young, couldn't sort out his feelings. Akram was familiar with this. He himself had once hero-worshipped Sajid. But he also knew, from his own experience, that the time would come when the young boy would start questioning, start to assert his authority. And then he would be useless. Look at Javed and Imran. One was stupid, the other sly. But both believed that they were equal to Feroze. The time wasn't far when they'd consider themselves equal to him as well. Then they'd become too dangerous and he would have to get rid of them somehow. Anyhow. Akram smiled as he fashioned a broom out of twigs and leaves. Aftab had once compared him to his mother. If only he could see him now. Doing a woman's work — housekeeping. But Akram was a fastidious man. He liked to keep things in order. Clean. He washed away the blood spilled from his recent kill. It wouldn't do to attract an inquisitive bear or wolf. Besides, it kept him limber and busy. But he could imagine Aftab leaping to do anything for his leader, even sweep a cave.

Yes, Aftab was different. He was more intelligent yet more trusting than the other two boys. More innocent. The problem with him was his attachment to his family. It was a problem. When the time came, would this bond make him weak? Would it make him question, or would his belief in his leader and his cause be strong enough to carry him through his actions? No matter what they were? No matter who it hurt?

And then there was Feroze. Akram loved him dearly. He was wise beyond his years because he'd suffered beyond his years. But, like an old man, he was also becoming softhearted. Treating the younger boys like brothers rather than jihadis in training. You had to teach these boys to depend on you completely, to take every order and carry it out blindly. When would he learn that it just doesn't pay to become so fond of each other? That's the first rule for a militant. Don't grow roots, don't develop bonds. Because then it becomes difficult to cut them and to let go when the time comes. As it will because it must.

Akram recalled the time, in his early days of training, Sajid had brought him a homeless puppy. He had cared for it, fed it, and was comforted by its warm little presence in his bed when he remembered the family he would never know again. And then, one day, Sajid had commanded him to kill the young dog. Akram, a young boy himself, begged his boss, swore he'd kill anything else, anything, but his beloved four-legged friend. But the command, once given, was never revoked. The puppy came bounding up, trusting eyes full of eager love for his master. The cold blade had torn into the young boy as much as it had into the heart of his pet. And he had wept inconsolably into Sajid Bhai's shoulder for hours, even days after it was over. But he understood later what his boss had been trying to teach him. In this world of theirs, death was just another part of life and there was no love greater than the cause they lived, and indeed, died for. So, when Sajid had brought another pet for him, a kitten this time, Akram had looked after it, but not let his heart get the better of him for he knew that it was only a matter of time when he would have to exterminate this little life too. And when the time had come, he hadn't shed a single tear, he had not begged for the cat to be allowed to live on. No tears, except, that night, when he had woken up to the sound of helpless mewing – lonely in the dark cold outside. Then he hadn't been able to stop his secret tears. He had crept outside and found a homeless stray begging to be loaned some love and warmth, but Akram had shooed it away. He would spare this life before it became a part of his. The cat had given him the same look of shocked betrayal as his pup and kitten had when he had done them in. Then he hadn't been able to stop his tears. But no one knew. And in the morning, his heart was steel.

But Feroze now, for all his belief in the cause, was becoming an impediment to action. He was too protective of the boys. Too afraid for them. He would always want to wait. Patience instead of action. And Akram had none of the former and believed in the latter. When the time came, he would have to get Feroze out of the way so that he wouldn't stop the boys from doing what needed to be done. He would do away with Feroze. Get him out. It would have to be done.

Akram sighed. The cost would be heavy, that much was certain. Whatever it was had to be done, whenever, there would be blood. Plenty of it. It was just a matter of whose. If anyone was watching, they would have seen a restless, brooding figure moving to the rhythm of his own thoughts, punishing his body with a series of hard exercises. But there was no one watching except the silent trees, the cloudless sky. So no one watched the restless musings of the man as he evolved a plan of action that would unleash a fresh spate of terror in the valley far below. And then, it was time to move.

9

Invisible eyes watched

Panic had seeped out and despondency crept in. Aftab was now completely bereft of ideas. He'd even gone to Imran and Javed's houses. But they weren't in. Nobody knew where they were or when they'd be back. At an emergency meeting. No doubt. An emergency that excluded him – or was it to do with him?

If it hadn't been for the beautiful brown dog that smilingly stayed by his side, he would probably have broken down and wept. It was nice of the two shepherds to have allowed the dog to stay with him for a little while.

Drawn by the sounds of a leather ball on the willow, Aftab found himself at the cricket pitch. Angad came charging up, his patka askew, his long hair escaping all over the place. His cheeks aflame with exertion and excitement.

'Arre yaar, Afti, where have you been? We need you, yaar, c'mon, we've no time to waste.'

Pretty soon, Angad had got Aftab at the bowler's end. In spite of himself, Aftab couldn't help smiling. It felt good that no one questioned his right to get first priority with the ball. It felt good to be wanted. By someone. The shadow of the morning darkened his eyes once again. But then, the excitement of the game, the sheer thrill of the feel of the leather ball fitting snugly in his hand forced Aftab back into the reality of being a young boy again.

Unknown to him, invisible eyes watched the progress of the game. Two hidden faces lit up with smiles of pleasure as a speedball sliced through the air and sent the middle stump spinning high into the air. The boy's whoops of delight carried through the air.

Major Ramneeq couldn't suppress a smile of delight. It pleased him to see the boy amongst others of his own age. Playing boys' games.

Far away from the damaging influence of violence and militants. Far away. His faraway son ... he tried to remember his face, his son's face. But, he realized with horror that he couldn't recall it. His own son's face. Instead, there was Aftab's face there. Where is my son? I want my son.

Stop. Put the thought away. Thoughts of his son would have to wait.

Akram too, on the opposite hill, couldn't suppress the smile of delight, as the middle stump obediently flew to the force of Aftab's ball. It pleased him to see the boy's deadly aim, accuracy and speed. It pleased him to see his shagirdh's flailing arms as he bore down on his retreating victim. No sympathy slowing his victorious leaps. He had the killer instinct. That was good. It would come in handy when the time came.

After the game was over, Angad flopped down next to Aftab. 'Great, that was great, Afti.'

'Yeah .... '

'But you are a bit out of practice, y'know .... '

'Fine, so get someone who's better,' Aftab snapped, knowing he was one of the best fast bowlers here.

'Look,' soothed Angad, worrying at the scab on his knee, as his mother always told him not to. 'Look, that's not what I mean – and you know it. You're the best bowler we've got, yaar, especially since Laxman Kachru's left with his family.'

'Left – where've they gone – for how long?'

'See, that's just what I mean. You've been out of circulation for so long. Don't you even know about Kachru's uncle?'

'No, which uncle?'

'Kachru Silk Stores wale uncle, yaar, you know him.'

'Sonu Mama? What happened to him?'

'He was driving in his Gypsy, see, and passing outside the Cantonment area. The driver went over an empty packet in the middle of the road. It blew up .... '

'An IED – outside the Cantt? What happened to Sonu Mama?'

'His legs blew off ....'

'Hai ....'

'And he lost a lot of blood. They've taken him to Delhi, or someplace, but, but they don't know if he'll survive.'

'Yah Allah! Poor guy, he's really a good man. So, what about Laxman – he has gone with his uncle? When'll he be back?'

'They've left, for good – I don't think they'll be back – at least not till things are better. Not for a l-o-n-g time, at least.'

'Just packed up and left? Just like that, without even saying goodbye?'

'He said goodbye. He came that night. But where the hell have you been? That's just my point, na? Recently, you have not been around for anyone to say hello to, or – or – goodbye.'

Aftab was silent. Too many things were going through his mind right now. First, first the loss of his friend and fellow bowler – without even saying goodbye. Sonu Mama – so badly hurt. Maybe even .... And who, who had planted the IED? Who was operating in and around this territory? This was their territory. Or – or was it Akram Bhai's planning? And he, Aftab, a member of the group, didn't even know? If he had known, he would never have let them plant the thing there. Why – it was just where all his friends lived. Param and ... and Angad.

'It was horrible, Afti – I – I saw it happen, right in front of my eyes. When the bomb went off, I saw a man fly, but his legs went the other way. Oh Aftab – it was right near my house. It could have been us, anyone of us. Afti, it was horrible, I'm – I'm scared. Suppose something like this was to happen to you, or me?

'Yes,' brooded Aftab to himself, what then? What if, instead of Sonu Mama, it had been Laxman himself, or Angad or – even closer home – his father – Shazia? His mother! He would have to stop Akram Bhai then. Explain that these people were close to him, they mattered to him.

'Don't worry Angu, I wouldn't have let anything happen to you …,' he thought.

'Kya – you wouldn't have let anything happen? Arre Afti, are you seeing dreams of grandeur or something? You think you've become Superman who'll fly down and save us all?' Angad burst out laughing and thumped a startled Aftab hard on the back.

'Huh?' Aftab sputtered, realizing with sudden horror that he had spoken out aloud. He was really being stupid now. Putting himself and Akram Bhai in great, great danger. Stupid, he scowled and kicked himself. Luckily, Angad was too pleased with his Superman joke to notice the emotions that coloured his friend's face.

They were now walking towards the market. Aftab was quiet. But his mind was not. Innumerable questions whirled within him.

He had to find out who had done this. One of them or one of us? If it were the first, then he'd have to warn

Akram Bhai. Somehow find him and warn him that there was someone encroaching on what was now acknowledged as their territory.

There was an unspoken understanding between the various groups operating in and around the Kashmir valley. Invisible lines webbed the valley, marking territories of operation. Had those invisible lines been broken – was it going to be a free-for-all now? He had to find out what was going on. He had to. A sharp bark brought him out of his reverie.

'Watch out,' shouted Angad, leaping out of the way as a big dog with a plumed tail came bounding up to them. 'Sheru, Sheru …,' laughed Aftab, throwing his arms around the dog, 'Look what you've done, you've frightened my friend. Angad, don't be scared, this is Sheru.'

'Kya, so now you have a dog of your own – that's what's been keeping you from us and your cricket practice?'

Aftab opened his mouth to say yes, that he had got a dog of his own. But then he saw the two gujjars, Sheru's real owners. 'Er – no – no, Sheru is their dog, we've just become friends.' The gujjars came up and the four of them got talking about how Sheru had been missing his new friend.

Up in the hidden hills, green eyes narrowed. Suspicion shone in them. These were the same men who'd been watching the game of cricket. Now they were here again. Were they – could they be keeping a watch on Aftab? Were they army men in disguise? Or militants of another group trying to lure him? Or trap him? A vein throbbed in Akram's throat. Something was amiss. He felt naked and exposed, even up here, sheltered by the green and rock. He'd have to make his move soon. The side which made the first move would win. The other would die. It was as simple as that.

10

Their dreams were souring before
their very eyes

Feroze saw the sign. 'At long last,' he sighed as he broke off the bent branch of the chir pine. This was the signal that only Akram and he knew. When they were unable to contact each other by any other means, the third branch of the third pine that edged the lake would be bent, till it was almost broken through. The recipient then broke off the twig completely to indicate that the message had been received. Feroze now inhaled the pungent smell of the freshly broken twig that lay in his hands. He was relieved to have the fall back sign that he'd been waiting for so anxiously. The silence after Akram's disappearance had been unbearable. He never knew where he went during these long dark periods of silence. And this time it had been worse because Feroze's body had deteriorated more than he could have ever imagined. He had not realized the extent to which his dependence on Akram had grown. Akram was almost an extension of his own self, the way he fulfilled his every little need from lighting cigarettes to mending his clothes. Now Feroze looked down at the cuff of his kameez, hanging loose at his wrist for the button had fallen off. And there was no way that he could even pick up a needle with his trembling hands, let alone thread it. And the tremors were worse because he couldn't light the cigarettes that helped calm him.

But that wasn't the worst. It had become imperative to contact Akram. Things had taken a turn for the worse. Their dreams were souring before their very eyes, and he didn't know how to stop the downward spiral. The chir snapped in Feroze's trembling fingers as he held onto it tightly, like a drowning man pulls down his rescuer. His mind swirled around the awful events of the last few days.

The IED planted in the cantonment area had not been daring, it had been rash and foolish. So stupid and pointless that it made Feroze suspicious. Who had been so stupid to risk so much, so close to the army's stronghold, just to kill one innocuous man and his driver? Certainly, insignificant people dying in the crossfire, well, that was just part of the job. But not like this when a small time shop-owner and his driver were the only victims. But there was worse to come.

As Feroze made his investigations into the IED blast as well as Akram's sudden disappearance, terrible truths were emerging. There was a connection being drawn between the blast and their outfit. It seemed that someone from amongst them had perpetrated the act. And now the army was going all out, sparing no effort in *'Nipping this new emerging gang in the bud ... '*, said the newspapers. 'Gang': as if they were a bunch of petty thieves. Not a 'militant outfit', the way they described the others. But who could it be? Not Akram Bhai; this wasn't his style at all. Akram's strikes were always aimed at a big impact affecting loads of people. Not this nothing raid of no consequence. Not worth the reaction that the army was having now. What was the point? And who had sanctioned the action, who had provided the arms? And who had carried out the orders?

Feroze was good at playing the mole. He could become as invisible as the air and he kept his silence well, overhearing, keeping his ear to the ground. But this time, what he found out was worse than he had imagined. The answer to his question – who had carried out the orders – was an uncomfortable one. It was Imran and Javed. Their own boys, their very own shagirdhs. But it wasn't on orders from Feroze or Akram, but from Sajid. The man both Akram and he had broken away from. And now, he had managed to break boys from their group. Taken revenge, and got the blame placed squarely on those whom he'd once worked with. And taken two of their little army. Two of whom Akram Bhai and he had worked hard to train. And how easily had these two little gaddaars broken away from the group they'd professed allegiance to. Gaddaars!! spat Feroze, hot with anger. It made his blood boil. Made his tremors worse.

Then he'd investigated the reasons behind the sudden disappearance of Akram and Aftab. He zeroed in on the old halwai. He heard, from his sources about how the man had flip-flopped his way to the nearest army post. How he'd tried to get Akram captured even while he tried to get some rest and tea. Feroze carefully watched Lala's coming and going. Yes, it had to be him. He had police protection now. He had something to hide. Well, thought Feroze, he couldn't hide forever. His fists clenched as he imagined himself throttling the fat man's oily neck. But he held his peace. He'd learned to be patient. He would wait for a sign from his brother.

And now, here it was. A signal at last. He would wait till later in the afternoon, when the school children were in the playground, to pick up the next part of the message. Just now, the ground was deserted; he would attract too much attention if he went in now. While he waited, he thought about the two gujjars who had struck up a conversation with young Aftab. Of course, right now, Aftab was too busy in his game of cricket. It was nice to see the boy with his friends, playing boys' games. Feroze had grown really fond of this child – a younger brother, a son, almost. Feroze had watched from the shadows as they played. But who were these shepherds? Were they keeping an eye on Aftab? Was this something to worry about? He wished Akram was here to talk to, to give voice to the worries and the enormity of their problems. Feroze wasn't used to being the decision-maker. And he desperately needed a cigarette now.

As the noon sun rose overhead, children began to gather in the warming park. Feroze smiled as he casually walked up to a group struggling to get their rusty old merry-go-round going. Offering his help, he was rewarded with their loud laughter as the swing went faster and faster. *Faster, faster,* they shouted, *faster, faster.* Feroze's laughter rose child-like with theirs.

His hands, arms felt stronger than they had for a long, long time. They were a blur of joy now, whipping the merry-go-round. Faster and faster.

Up in the trees, Akram smiled. It had been a long time since poor Feroze had laughed – almost since he'd lost his childhood and adopted the life of a man. 'Let him enjoy himself for a little while,' sighed Akram, 'Let him enjoy for both of us.' He rubbed the stiffness at the back of his neck and turned away.

But as he turned, his eyes widened in horror. For another laughing group was approaching the playground. Young Aftab, his Sikh friend, the dog. And the two shepherds. Who were they? What was their interest in Aftab? Why weren't they busy with their own work? Why were they in town for so long and not up in the pastures with their sheep? Indeed, where were their sheep? The questions ate at Akram's peace of mind. Vultures. Vultures of questions – pecking, irritating. This was not a good turn of events. If Aftab saw Feroze now, he would start, give himself away. To whom? Who were these men who hung on to the boy and pretended they were poor shepherds? They were not. That much was painfully obvious now, to Akram at least. They were someone else, they were in disguise. But were they army men or a couple of preying scouts from another jihadi outfit?

'Fasterfasterfaster' shouted the children. But Feroze put up his hands, 'Bas, bas ...,' he laughed, panting. With a final push, 'No, no – please, Bhai, please, be a sport,' the little ones insisted. 'I'll do it,' said another voice. Younger, but far more serious. Feroze's hands trembled and he clutched at the bars of the merry-go-round. A look. Brief, intense. Questioning. Then the older man turned away with a mumbled, 'Shukriya,' leaving Aftab to spin the swing, silently, solemnly. The shepherds stiffened imperceptibly. What was this look, this exchange? Was this a chance encounter or had the boy been out looking for this – this shaking leaf of a man? They took in his face, his build, his every gesture. Drinking in every detail in order to regurgitate it. Perhaps, after all this time, the cold trail was warming up. At least a little?

The hidden animal movements up on the hillside grew stiller. But with tension. Not calmness. The fists clenched with impotent frustration. He hated to be a helpless onlooker, when things were becoming more volatile by the minute. Akram's temples throbbed with growing anxiety as Feroze made his way trembling to the broken swing by the edge of the ground. The one with the two hollow tubes. One horizontal, one vertical. The ones that rested on each other. The ones in whose hearts the two parts of the message would be buried.

Surely Feroze wouldn't be stupid enough to take out the messages with so much obvious danger about.

Feroze stroked the broken bars of the swing as though it was a loved one. Briefly, but warmly. Fingers itched to retrieve the secrets that lay there, but he turned and sank to the ground, leaning against one of the bars. His fingers fumbled in his pocket where the comfort of cigarettes lay uselessly. He watched Aftab swing the children and smiled. He had done well to hide his surprise.

Aftab looked pointedly away from Feroze, although every fibre of his being yearned to go over to him, to re-establish links. To find out. To know where his, their, Akram Bhai was. But he kept his eyes averted, only occasionally glancing over. Only occasionally allowing his heart to melt at the sight of the fingers shakingly caressing the cigarettes within their box. Aftab knew well Feroze Bhai's desperate need for them. And knew now that Akram Bhai was not there to light up for him, to soothe his trembling. Aftab glanced away, blinking back tears.

The shepherds noticed too and one, with an imperceptible nod to his accomplice, ambled over to the fellow who sat on the ground.

'Salaam wallehkum, my brother ...,' flicking out a beedi, noting the flicker of longing in the other's eyes.

'Wallehkum salaam.' Tight, not a greeting, much less an invitation. Now here was a fellow who had something to hide.

'Beedi?' The longing again, the wry smile, as he held up his hands. 'Shukriya, but ... .' The lighted beedi passed between them, one noting that the other could barely hold onto it. Feroze's eyes rested on the hands that generously offered him the smoke. The woodsmoke eyes took in the fact that though the hands were hard and used to rough work, they were not the hands of a shepherd. *They were not the hands of a shepherd.*

The shepherd withdrew his hand and watched as the other closed his eyes which were now full of suspicion. Lost for a brief moment in the relief as he sucked the acrid smoke deep into his lungs.

'Bad hands, brother, what happened?'

'I was born with it,' the lie, well practiced, rolled off his tongue. He didn't even think about it, concentrating, instead, on the calming effect of the beedi. He'd have another – he'd offer one of his cigarettes to this man, whoever he was, he'd ask him to light one for him. Only, he'd have to keep his silence. But the shepherd had noted that the accent, though trying to be, was not from these parts. He was an Afghan, this shaking man.

'Bad hands, I wonder what happened?' asked the second shepherd, placing his hand on Aftab's shoulder, and indicating Feroze with a tilt of his head. 'Who knows, who cares,' shrugged Aftab, smiling within; he was getting better at this. At last.

'Poor fellow,' added the shepherd to the boy. Gently trying to probe. 'Probably a drunk, or drug addict, no? Look at the way he's enjoying my brother's beedi.'

Angad, bored by now, hiccupped loudly and reeled and swayed around, pretending to be a drunk.

'Ai, stop it, Angu, don't make fun of someone else's misfortune,' muttered Aftab, throwing a look of embarrassed apology towards Feroze. The children laughed and clapped for Angu, asking for more. And Angad, enjoying himself hugely, doubled his efforts, now perfectly mimicking Feroze's shaking limbs.

Aftab couldn't be the diplomat any longer. He had to take Akram Bhai's place. He had to protect Feroze from ridicule of any sort. He had to honour Feroze's valiant heroism that had caused these tremors. Perhaps it was just such a situation that Akram had spoken of when he'd said, 'I need someone to know.'

He did what he imagined Akram Bhai would have done. He strode up to his friend and dealt him a blow across the back of his head. Angad, trying to get away, lost his balance and fell on the shepherd, who fell on Aftab who in turn, toppled onto the rotating merry-go-round, hitting his head as the bars came around. 'Ah!' and there was blood.

The children screamed and leaped off the swing, crowding around, shouting, 'Blood, blood, he's bleeding! Look! He's bleeding.'

The shouts and the sight of blood shocked Angad into stillness. The shepherd pushed forward, to slow and stop the swing. The other shepherd leaped up too, shouting, 'The boy's hurt,' and he raced to the crowding children. Feroze stood up too, his sense of unease and suspicion rattling inside like heavy armour. The shepherd's speed of response, his athletic run towards the crowd was not that of a mountain goatherd. There was a betrayal of training in the movement. Army or jihadi training, he couldn't tell. But all was not well. He himself hesitated a moment, dragging on the last of the beedi, so close that it burned his fingers. Should he go to Aftab? Would the boy be able to pretend that they didn't know each other? Would he himself, if the boy was badly hurt? Then it occurred to him this was the moment. All eyes, all attention was on the accident. He could retrieve the message now. He slipped his fingers into one hollow tube. Held his breath to still the tremors. His fingers closed on the precious paper. Now the second.

11

Faster and faster it went
out of control

The playful mimicking of his dear Feroze had set Akram's blood boiling. As though he was transmitting his anger into his shagirdh, he saw Aftab take on his friend. He saw the fall, he sensed, more than heard, the children's shouts of blood, blood. He knew that it might be serious when he saw the shepherd sprint in a military man's response. Oh what had happened to the boy?

And then his heart stopped. The world stopped. For he saw that Feroze was retrieving the message with the plan on it. He saw one of the shepherds detach himself from the group of children. He saw him assess what Feroze was up to. He saw him move with trained speed towards him.

Almost without thinking, Akram ran down the slope, he could no longer be a bystander in this desperate turn of events.

Blood from his forehead was trickling into his eye. Aftab could taste the blood and it made his entire being spin. For a moment he thought that the merry-go-round was still spinning. Faster and faster it went around out of control. And he shouted. 'Stop it, stop it!!'

'I'm sorry, sorry, yaar.' That was Angad. Tearing off his putka, wiping the blood. 'It's alright, it's a small cut. Don't worry, don't worry.' He himself looked around for assurance, but only the little anxious faces of the flushed children surrounded them. Where were those two shepherds? Where had they suddenly disappeared? Couldn't they see that their friend needed help?

'Put your hands up and turn around very slowly.' The voice behind him made Feroze's legs buckle. Again, not again. He couldn't go through all that again. He turned. But as he turned, he tried to stuff the message into his mouth. For this was evidence, this was their plan. Rough hands pulled him. Dragged him down to the ground. 'Bas, bahut ho gaya, get down, get down on the ground.' Without even looking up, he could smell the familiar sour smell of gun grease. It was over, he was caught. Again. Akram, his mind sang – a silent prayer. 'Akram, Akram Bhai.' Would he save him again? Before the torture. He couldn't take torture anymore. Akram, Akram Bhai.

Akram stopped dead in his tracks, hugging a sturdy pine to absorb the thudding of his heart. There was a jeep racing to the broken gate. An army jeep .... All was lost. Feroze was lost. He couldn't take more torture now.

Major Ramneeq had just got the message on his wireless that he'd been anxiously waiting for. 'Suspected militant apprehended.' Ah! That was music to his ears. After weeks and months of almosts, there was finally one fish in the net. Big or small, he didn't know as yet. But he'd find out, soon enough. He was going to love finding out. He sprinted to where his men stood, revolvers aimed at the figure lying prone on the ground.

And then he saw it. A movement, up on the hillside. Somebody was lurking there, watching. He grabbed his Captain's rifle and looked through the lens. A shadow had melted behind a tree. A bush still shook with recent movement. Someone was up there. Interested in the goings-on below.

'Dhruv, up there – Captain Vyas,' he barked the order to one of the shepherds who was already stripping off the voluminous phiran that had effectively concealed all that he needed now in this moment of action. 'Up there, there's someone watching. After him, quick. Be careful.' A parting shot before they were out of earshot. The dog galloping ahead in response to a sharp whistle.

Blood. There was blood. Red, the red smell of blood. What was happening? Aftab was dizzy. Something was not right. Or was it terribly wrong? 'Angad, Angad yaar – kya ho raha hai – I'm, I'm not okay ....' 'It's okay, it's okay Aftab Bhai – just a small cut. Stand, just try to stand. That's right, slowly. Slowly now. Here put your arm around my shoulder. Oof tu kitna mota ho gaya hai, yaar – I can't lift you, you're way too fat for me. Wait, where are those shepherd friends of yours?'

His gasp and 'Oi' of surprise forced Aftab out of himself – 'Kya? Kya hua?' He followed his friend's gaze and the moan that escaped his lips made Angad spin around, thinking his friend had fainted. He almost had.

'Wh-what's happening, Angad, why's that nice man on the ground? Is he hurt? Why aren't they helping him?'

As Angad confirmed his worst fears, Aftab was filled with remorse, guilt, almost. Had it been his fault? Had he, somehow, put Feroze Bhai into this danger? What would happen now? Would they arrest Feroze – on what grounds? Would they, would they, torture him? He couldn't take more torture now. Torture. The word conjured up more blood. His own blood mingled with Feroze's. And then it occurred to him. Perhaps he himself was in danger now. Would Feroze's arrest lead somehow to his own? Was Feroze Bhai really strong enough to withstand brutal army questioning? Or would he say 'That boy, he's the one – one of us …!'

'Angad, Angad, let's get out of here. It's not safe. Let's go.'

But for Angad this was real excitement. At long last. After months of curfews, bandhs and warnings to stay quietly indoors, here was some excitement and action at last. 'Maybe this is the fellow responsible for Sonu Mama's accident – what do you say?' Angad asked, his hair loose and long, echoing his excitement.

'NO!' Aftab's answer was quick and sharp. Sure. Angad gave him a sharp look of his own. But further questions were quelled for now as a strapping figure in military fatigues strode up to them.

'So, young friend, tum yahan bhi?' The Major was picking Aftab up and examining the cut above the eyebrow. It was still bleeding. He looked at the blood-soaked patka and smiled at the flush-faced boy whose hair flowed down his back.

'Are you with him?' 'Yes sir,' the boy almost saluted him in excitement. The merry eyes, the flushed cheeks. His son. His faraway son. Yearning flooded the Major. In spite of himself. He tousled the boy's curly hair, before turning back to examine the other's cut. 'Was it him that hit you again? Have they been after you again?' Without looking up, Aftab knew he was indicating Feroze Bhai.

'No!' Again. Too quick. Too sure. 'Well,' thought the Major, 'He knows him, or something about him, that's for sure.'

'What's this?' wondered Angad. Uneasy suddenly. The Major seemed to know something about his friend, that even he didn't know — who had been after Aftab?

Angad quickly told the story of how his friend got the cut on his head. Well, that itself was simple and straightforward enough. But it was still strange that the boy had just happened to be in the very same park as this militant. And who was hiding up in the hills? And this Sikh boy — where did he fit in?

'I want you both to come with me,' ordered the Major. The militant was already being hauled towards the jeep. 'But uncle, sir,' began Angad. 'Tie your hair up, this is no way for a Sikh boy to be running around,' was the Major's reply as he touched his own turban. He could barely resist not reaching out to give the worried little boys a reassuring hug. But he didn't. The militant was shoved into the back seat of the jeep first, with the shepherd next to him. Angad was getting in next, but the Major held him back and told Aftab to get in first. Then Angad, who tried, in vain, to knot up his unruly hair. The Major got in the front seat. No one noticed as he adjusted the side view mirror.

Up on the hillside, shots were fired, the sounds ricocheting off the rocks. Then there were answering shots from two other weapons. Ramneeq nodded and smiled.

'They've killed him,' he said. Loud enough. And noted that the militant and Aftab's heads jerked up to look towards the direction of the sounds, their eyes widened in horror. He also noticed that the Sikh boy didn't know much of what was going on.

Aftab, his heart racing, breaking, was acutely aware of the terrible shaking of Feroze Bhai's legs next to him. He longed to take on Akram Bhai's role. Akram would have known what to do. Even in these terrible circumstances. He would have found a way to reassure his friend. Aftab glanced sideways, as Feroze's hand slipped off his leg. Cautiously, Aftab slipped his own hand down and covered the shaking one with his own. His thumb, caressing, soothing. He hoped.

Angad was shocked at this little gesture his friend thought was hidden from view. What on earth was this? Was Afti known to this fellow? Did he share some affinity with the wretch? Almost against his will, a clearer picture was emerging in Angad's mind. Afti's absences, his silence, his saying that he wouldn't let anything happen to Angad or his family. The way he'd flared up at his mimicking this fellow. The way he seemed so sure that this man was not the one responsible for the Kachru explosion. Angad stared at Aftab as though at a stranger. A hated stranger. But all he saw was his dearest friend. Perturbed, he looked away and met the eyes of the Major in the mirror. The Major nodded, smiled. Trying to reassure the lad. But the look also showed that he had seen the caressing hand too. And he didn't like it either.

The Cantonment gates swung open. The Major left some instructions with the guard. And then ordered the driver to drive straight to the holding area.

Were they under arrest?

12

Free them if he could. Kill them
if he must

Blood. There was blood everywhere. The rushing river sucked at the wound like a hungry demon. But the ice numbed the pain. And that was good. And it would throw the dog off the scent.

Akram looked back. Yes, the river was swift enough to disperse the red and not leave a condemning trail for his pursuers to follow. He would not be caught. He would not. His work was not yet done. Why, it had barely begun. And he would free Feroze and Aftab. Free them if he could. Kill them if he must. At any cost. But for now, all he could do was to stay ahead of his pursuers. The barking of the dog warned him that it was back on his trail.

Akram was a creature of the mountains. He could outwit a snow leopard, if he needed to. He found a pool looping out from the river, part of it, yet apart.

Overhanging rocks and creepers sheltered it. He pulled up some reeds, quickly bound his shattered leg in a tight tourniquet and disappeared with the faintest ripple under the water. He sucked on one end of the hollowed reed. Slowly. Using the little air to bring his pounding heart back under strict control. But the leg had turned cold now. A part, a precious part of him, was dying.

Blood. There was blood everywhere. There were teeth lying loose in his mouth, but he wouldn't give his captors the satisfaction of spitting them out with his blood.

He gave them no satisfaction by way of answers either. And he couldn't suppress the smile when they puzzled over the message – the half message. It made no sense if you didn't have the other half. Even to him, well, only partly. So there was very little that he could give them. Except. Except, he couldn't control the cry of pain when the blow landed on his cheek again. Where was Aftab, he wondered? Then banished the thought, banished the child's name right out of his mind, lest his tongue loosened and gave the enemy the name. The connection.

Once, only once, did he give himself the satisfaction, the sukoon, the peace of mind of conjuring up Akram Bhai's face, name, fiery eyes. Yah Allah! Akram mere bhai, don't be dead, please, please, don't be dead. Without you I am dead. We're all dead. He embraced the thought of his soul brother once tightly to his heart. And then he let him go. As he slipped into the velvet softness of black blankness. All else faded. Was irrelevant.

Blood. There was blood everywhere. The doctor was examining the wound. But the blood wouldn't stop. 'Stitches, I'm afraid,' he pronounced and brought out needle and injections and smells that made the frightened boy faint and dizzy.

Angad was on the phone with his parents, pouring out a garbled, excited version of the afternoon's events with one of the military men taking furious notes. He smiled, the story seemed like one from a cheap film, but the parents at the other end were frantic with worry. Naturally.

Unable to take the frightened cries of pain of the young Aftab, Major Ramneeq came to the room where the other rattled the story to his parents. Gently he took the phone from him and spoke to the parents himself.

'Satsriakalji,' he began and then went on to explain that he knew that their son was innocent, but that he had been at the scene when the suspected militant was captured. He only needed to ask Angad a few questions. 'He's completely safe, prahji, not to worry, he is just like my son.' His throat tightened, he shut his eyes against the pain of the loss of his son. 'I will have him escorted home by plainclothesmen. He is a good boy, I know, and a brave one. Yes, the other one, Aftab, no-no. He's not in any trouble. Just questions prahji, he helped us nail this fellow. No, no, nothing that will endanger the boys ....'

A thousand reassurances later, and finally, he was able to get back to the job at hand. But as he turned to Angad, he found the boy in tears. Now that the excitement had poured out, the realization of actual danger came creeping in. That, and the cries of pain from both sides of the corridor. The militant's on the one side where he was being 'questioned'. And Aftab's on the other, where the wound was being stitched.

'I'm sorry,' he sobbed into the Major's chest, 'I'm sorry, it's all my fault.' It took time and patience and hot cups of thick, sweet tea to explain to Angad that it wasn't his fault at all. It was as it should have been. If he had not pushed Aftab, the militant would not have tried using the moment to retrieve the secret message. Then he wouldn't have been caught. They hadn't yet deciphered the entire message, but they knew that it was a plan for a big terrorist strike of some sort. So, by causing his friend a small cut, a little loss of blood, a little pain, Angad had, in fact, saved many lives. That cheered him up a little, was he a hero, then – finally? But still the thought haunted him – what of Aftab's connection? It haunted them both. Both had hinted at their unease. But neither wanted to reveal their hand. As yet.

That there was a connection, there was little doubt now, but what, how much? Angad couldn't bear the thought, so he wept instead, and made up his mind that he wouldn't voice his misgivings to the Major, he would go directly to Afti – find out for himself. And help his dear friend out of the sticky web in which he now found himself caught.

13

The truth now,
what's been going on

Aftab was startled out of his dreams. He was exhausted, sweating. He'd spent his sleep running, running, running to catch up with shadows. But they kept merging and separating until he wasn't sure how many they were and which one was he to chase.

He started as his mother tried to wipe the sweat from his bruised, aching forehead. 'It's alright, meri jaan, Nooro. You're home, it's alright.' And she spooned tea into his mouth. 'You sleep, beta, rest yourself, you've had a bad fright. See, your Abbu has already gone to get liver for you. I'll cook it tender, just the way you like it. You've lost so much blood, na? The liver will help you, give you strength. But for now, just rest, beta. Does your head hurt a lot? The doctor said you needed four stitches. Bechara, mera Nooro ...,' she clucked on like a loving hen and Aftab reveled in it, soothed out of his nightmares, forgetting for a little while the troubled questions that lay ahead. He was lulled into sleep again. Ammi waited a while and watched. She had questions of her own to ask. Where had he been, why was he becoming so moody, so secretive, why was he wherever these badmash firangis were? But she saw the need for peace on her son's brow and she thought, 'Later, I'll ask him later.' *She didn't know then, that later would be too late.*

The next thing he knew, Angad was by his bed, shaking him awake, 'Uth, uth, Afti – we have to talk. You've had enough rest.'

'Oh ho, let me sleep,' moaned Aftab, rolling over, touching his bandages for good effect. He didn't want to face Angad and the inevitable questions he could hear hovering about him. 'Suno, I'm sorry yaar, about your head, I mean. Does it hurt a lot?'

'Idiot, then what? Of course it hurts, burns – want me to give you one to see what it feels like?'

'Acha, sorry, mere yaar – but there was no need for you also to react like that – na? After all, you hit me too, na? How did I know that you'd become such a softie that you'd keel over the minute I just touched you?'

'Touched me? Wait, you just wait, I'll touch you and let's see how steady you can be.' Aftab leaped out of bed and chased Angad out of the house. Ammi smiled, yes, this is how it should be with little boys, chasing each other, laughing. In relief, she began to light up the stove to make some hot pakoras for them, calling out to Shazia to help cut onions and potatoes.

Outside, their horsing around came to an abrupt halt. Aftab tried to carry it on, knowing what was to follow, but his head hurt. 'Okay Afti, the truth now, what's been going on?' Angad was not one to beat around the bush.

Aftab sighed and sat on the ground, resting his back against the wall. As always, he didn't quite know what he was going to say. Or how he was going to stem the flow of curious questions. For lack of any other ideas, bereft of energy to think up new ones and heartsick at the terrible turn of events, Aftab shut his eyes and once again let his tongue speak the lies that Shazia had placed in his head. 'They were after Shazia Aapa. They threatened to abduct her. I had to pay them off to prevent that. I was negotiating the amount ....'

This was the third time he was condemning Akram Bhai with his lying tongue. The third time the lies spilled out. But each time it became harder instead of easier. For this time, for all he knew, he could be speaking ill of the dead. And Allah would never forgive him for that.

Tears escaped from the corners of his eyes, so he covered his face with his hands. Ashamed of his lies, his tears, his betrayals to all his friends, this side and that. He felt utterly, utterly alone. This was not how things were supposed to have happened. He had been ready for heroism, not for this, this ....

Angad looked at his friend and knew that there wasn't truth in his words. There were too many holes in the story. Most importantly, why had he wanted to protect that militant, and why had he held his hand to comfort him? He would never have done that if this were a man who was threatening to abduct his sister. He wanted to know the truth. He had to. That was the only way he could help his friend, save him.

'Dekh Afti,' he leaned over, put his arm on the other's shoulder and whispered. 'Dekh dost, you can't hide the truth from me – I'm sure you have very good reasons for lying ... but I know that you are lying.'

'Oh ho, what's the matter with you? As though I'd make up such a story – about Shazia Aapa, at that ....'

'Ah, do I hear my name?' and there she was holding a plate of steaming hot pakoras. 'What khusar pusar are you two doing about me?'

'Ah ha, Aapa, pakoras, yummy.' Angad made a great show of biting into one, rolling his eyes, smacking his lips, until Shazia gave him a friendly clout on his head. 'Stop your drama. Just because your friend is a complete idiot, doesn't mean his sister is one too. Now stop pretending and tell me what were you two talking about.'

'I, I'll tell you later, Aapa, it – it's about yesterday.' Aftab tried to put off the conversation. But Angad didn't want Shazia to go just yet; it wasn't often that he had a chance to be near her. She was the most beautiful girl he had ever seen.

'Okay, Aapa, listen, it's about yesterday. There's something really strange going on with this fool here.

He's trying to feed me with all kinds of lies. But you and I know that he's just telling lies. I can't figure out why, but I intend to find out. Aapa,' he leaned closer to her, 'I think we need to help him whether he wants our help or not.'

'Why d'you say he's lying, Angu Bhai?' Shazia smiled her dazzling smile at him, melting his heart, she knew, popping another pakora into his mouth. Aftab shot her an angry look, why did she have to behave like this in front of his friends? 'Kyon Angad, what makes you say that his story of trying to save my izzat is lies?'

'You know about this? Is it true then?'

'I don't know — you tell me, you seem sure it's not. You must tell me Angad, you must tell me all that you know, all that you saw, all that you told those military walas,' she persuaded him, using every weapon in a woman's armory — smiles, looks, anxious fluttering — and he told her everything he knew. Although he had planned to keep this a man-to-man thing, between Aftab and himself, he even divulged every detail of yesterday's events. Why, even his unspoken suspicions that he'd kept secret from the Major, were now in the possession of the beautiful, green-eyed Shazia.

And when it was done and there was no more to be said, she packed him off with a sisterly hug and told him not to worry anymore.

She would handle it all, now.

She turned to her brother. He looked up sullenly at her. She regarded him for a few moments, weighing the facts, wondering which track to take.

'Aftab,' she began, deciding to be as grave and serious as the situation demanded, 'My Chottey Boey, he is full of questions and suspicions, this friend of yours, what are you going to do about it?'

At first Aftab tried going for his usual: there's no need to do anything, it'll all go away. But for once he knew that it wasn't going away just like that. 'I don't know, Aapa. I didn't think he'd notice so much.'

'No, of course you didn't,' she said gently, persuading him to take one of the now cold pakoras, 'But that's the trouble, no, Boey? You mustn't ever underestimate the intelligence of the other side.'

'He isn't the "other side", Aapa, he is my friend. He's like my own brother.'

'Your friend, ah yes, Aftab, your brother. But remember this, for now and for as long as you live. In this path you have chosen for yourself, there are no friends, or family, even. No one is to be treated with anything less than suspicion. Haven't you learned anything from Akram and Feroze Bhai?'

She smiled as he gasped, 'Aapa, how …?'

'How do I know? I know them too, Aftab. Your path is my path.'

'But, but how? You're just a girl, you hardly go out. And how come Akram Bhai never told me. He … he told you about me?'

'I've known about your involvement from the very beginning, Boey, because my involvement came first, before yours. And Nooro, mere Bhai, don't be angry now. Akram never told you about me because he wasn't sure how you'd react. He loves you dearly.'

'And I him!' asserted Aftab hotly.

'And I him!' said Shazia softly.

And then all went quiet.

Aftab struggled with this new information. What did Aapa mean? Surely … surely not? She waited, saw his struggle, then went on to explain, 'We've been together, as man and wife, for nearly two years now, Aftab. We love each other …,' she waited, 'Do you mind, Aftab?' There was a film of tears in her eyes and voice.

Aftab didn't know how to answer this question – did he mind? Yes, he did mind. She was his sister – his sister. And … and Akram's life was not the life he wanted for his sister. A life of uncertainty. Danger. And why was this kept from him, by both of them? Two years, almost two years they'd kept this secret from him? Ammi had become suspicious of him, but for so long, Shazia Aapa had evaded even Ammi's prying eyes. Why, they were trying to arrange a marriage for her, they are on the lookout for a groom. And, were they … .

'Are you married, Aapa?'

'Not formally, no. You understand, don't you, we can't have a nikaah ceremony, who would perform it?

112

And Akram — he lives a shadow life, he cannot come out in the open and get married. But we will soon, as soon as we can, Inshahallah.' The tears came then, for soon seemed very faraway. 'We are like man and wife, Boey, he treats me with a lot of respect.'

'Would Ammi-Abbu allow it?'

'I don't know — probably not. You know how Ammi is about the firangis.' She said it gently, with a smile, with love in her voice. It was the first time he had heard the word said like that, in a way that wasn't a curse. She turned towards the house and they both saw Ammi looking out at them. She waved and they waved back.

'She's happy,' Aapa laughed, 'She thinks I'm helping bring sense into that silly head of yours.' She was about to push his head away with her fingertips, but instead let them linger on the bandage.

'Does it hurt a lot, tell me what happened?'

And she heard the tale again, this time from her brother's point of view. Angad had put it in the Major's words. Aftab now realized that it was because of his fall that Feroze Bhai had thought it safe to extricate the message and then had been caught with evidence. 'It is my fault, Aapa, isn't it?'

'No, Aftab, that's not your fault. But what you should have done is to ignore Feroze Bhai, not hold his hand in the army jeep. I know,' she held up her hand as he started to protest, 'I know it must have been difficult with poor Feroze Bhai shaking so much, but you could have pretended that you didn't know him. Your gesture brings you under clearer suspicion. But anyway, it's done now. We'll think of some way out.' *And Shazia, as always, did.*

'So what now, Aapa?' He couldn't voice it, but the sounds of the shots from the wooded hillsides and the Major's smug statement, 'They've killed him,' stabbed like a sword into him.

'There were shots, Aapa,' he choked, 'The Major said ....'

'He lives,' her smile was bright, her eyes brighter with tears. 'He's been hurt, shot. But he lives.'

They hugged each other then, in a tight embrace, weeping their hearts out. Together.

Ammi, standing at the window was puzzled. What was going on? But Shazia was the sensible one, she'd set things right. She was confident of that. She feared for her Nooro, though. He was hotheaded and his heart was filled with firangi poison. She'd tell Shazia to persuade him to drop this company.

There was enough time later, much later, to regret that she had left it all up to her daughter.

'How do you know, Aapa?'

'Boey, I can't tell you – it's dangerous for you. Please don't ask.'

'You've met him, seen him yourself. Since then?'

A long pause. The barest nod.

'You'll see him again?'

Nod. A whisper, 'We can't live without each other.'

Aftab smiled, 'Aapa, no, I don't.'

'Don't what?'

'You asked me before, do I mind. About Akram Bhai and you. No, I don't mind. I only ….'

'Wish you'd known? Yes?'

'Yes.'

'There were many reasons, Chottey, your own safety, most of all. Also, I told Akram that I'd persuade you, but he knows that you're very protective of me and you may not have liked it.'

He laid his head in her lap and she stroked his head. There were so many questions, so many things to be done. Their cause. But, for now, most immediately, they were bound together by their need for the green-eyed man who lay hidden, wounded. Alone. They comforted each other as though they were comforting the one who wasn't there, whom they couldn't.

'Shazia Aapa, I want to meet him. Please.'

'Aftab, I don't know, it's very dangerous.'

'If you can, I can. Aapa please, don't deny me this. See, now there's no one else. What with Feroze Bhai in jail and Javed and Imran, who knows where, and Akram Bhai hurt and in hiding …. See, I'm the only one who can do something. But I need him to tell me what. I can't just wait around.'

After a long silence, Aapa said, 'I'll ask him. I'll tell him all that has happened. And we have to try and think of how we, you and I, can help Feroze Bhai.'

'Dakiya,' a call and rattle at the gate disturbed them. Ammi called out, 'Aiyee, Shazia kuri – stop lazing

115

now, get the letters and then come in – there's work to be done.'

'Oof,' sighed Shazia, 'Always calling me to work.'

'Wait Aapa, I'll get it. I'll do it for you.'

'For me? Or for your Akram Bhai, huh?'

'For both.' They smiled. But Amir had got to the gate first. 'Oi Aftab Bhai, look, a letter for you. From Dilli.'

14

Refugees

Dear Aftab Bhai,

   Salaam wallehkum!

   How are you? And your family? Give my regards to everyone.

   This letter has been in my heart for a long, long time. I've written it many times over, but this is the first time I'm putting pen to paper.

   I wanted so much to meet you before we left Baramullah. But Angu and I just didn't know where you were, or where to find you. Where have you been hiding? Do you have a girlfriend, now? That's what Angu said, so don't get angry with me for saying that.

   But you probably know by now about our sudden departure after the blast in which Sonu Mama was hurt. Oh Aftab, it was just horrible. Faroukh Bhai had been our driver for so long. He was killed instantly. But maybe he was luckier than Sonu Mama who really suffered. Both his legs were blown off as the bomb exploded right under the jeep. He was thrown up in the air. In the fall, he also badly fractured, oh so many bones. You just can't imagine. He was in so much pain. In the Srinagar hospital they gave him blood, and tied him up. He was just a ball of bandages. They told us that he'd die. So Abbu and Ammi and Santosh Mami talked the entire night and by morning it was decided: we would leave Kashmir by the earliest flight. All of us – full family. When I started to cry that I didn't want to go, they told me that it was just for a little while. Just until things got better. But as the days pass, I see more clearly that there may be no coming back for us.

Sonu Mama lived about a week, but the suffering was too much and he died. Santosh Mami, Chandan and Chanchal still cry all the time. We're all living in one room in an ashram. Abbu says we've become refugees.

Refugees? Like when India and Pakistan were separated? But there's no partition here – then why are we refugees – in our own country? I don't understand, Aftab. And there are so many other Kashmiri Pandits here. All of them have such terrible stories to tell – you can't even imagine. Almost everyone has lost family members and property, money, jobs. But it isn't only Kashmiri Pandits, I try to tell them. Everyone, everyone has suffered, but no one wants to listen. Vipin says that he'd like to kill every Kashmiri he meets. He says, why should they get to live in the comfort of their home when we are denied the same? I tried to tell him that it isn't every Kashmiri. It isn't our friends, it's only the enemy, the firangis and those who've chosen to join them. I tell him that we are Kashmiris too, the Kashmiri Pandits are Kashmiris as much as the Muslims are, and that they are our brothers. It is the antankvadis, the gun-toting terrorists who are the enemy. Our common enemy. But he isn't ready to listen just now, just tells me to shut up or he'll kill me instead of the Kashmiris. My mother keeps telling me to shut up too. People here have forgotten, or want to forget that they are Kashmiris too. People are getting used to life here, even if it is so hard, so awful. I don't want to get used to it, to this. So I just had to write this letter to you. I had to share this with somebody. I hope you understand. Because I can feel the conviction leaving me sometimes, I'm afraid I'll start thinking like Vipin and the others, if I don't get through to you. If you don't understand, if you don't believe, agree.

Yesterday, the news came that someone had broken into our Kachru Silk Store and stolen cloth and other stuff. They said that someone was even living there! There were signs of someone cooking. There, in our lovely, posh shop. My father says that he's lost everything, everything. He keeps saying this and that makes Santosh Mami and her twins cry more. I asked him when we could go back home and he beat his fist against his head and said that I should forget that Kashmir was ever my home. He says this is home now. But Aftab, there's nothing here to call home. Ammi says that it'll get better. She says she's trying to find a school for all of us here. That it'll be a regular school which is open when it should be, not closed all the time like our schools back home. I couldn't say it to her, of course, but you, me and Angu know that it's much more fun in a closed school than an open one, no? Now Ammi has said that I should stop calling them Ammi-Abbu. She says Pitaji and Mataji are better. Better how? I can't suddenly change what I've been calling them all my life, but she says I have to try.

I long for home, Afti. I want to come back to Baramullah. It's hot here and crowded and I feel more frightened here than back home, even after all that has happened.

I HATE these militants, all of them. The firangis and those among us who've joined them to become monsters who hunger for our blood, our peace of mind. After what's happened to Sonu Mama, I really wish that I could kill these terrorists – militants, monsters. When I said this aloud the other day, Abbu slapped me and told me that there'd been enough killing. What I don't understand, how can he say that, even after Sonu Mama. I don't care, I really wish I could kill just one of these jaanwars.

Afti, I wanted to warn you, to caution you. Be very, very careful of these fellows. They look like us, like human beings, but they're not. And they have no iman, no dharm, no religion. They pretend they have a cause, but they're only serving themselves – using us. Abbu says they're preying like animals on young boys, making them join their false cause with promises of money or heaven or something. Don't be taken in by any of this, Afti, they are evil. Stay far away from them. They'll kill anyone and everyone. We're all in danger of them and they'll drive stakes between us Afti. I never wanted to leave, but I had to – probably forever. You and I, we've never thought that I'm a Kashmiri Pandit, you're a Muslim or that Angu's a Sikh. I was thinking about this last night. How we never thought of our differences – we were a bit like those national integration stories and plays they keep making us do in school, no? But they, Afti, they're making us think like that – different. Believe me. I sit and hear the way the others around me have started thinking and talking. It was never like this. Believe me, there'll come a time when we will start finding differences between ourselves too.

If we don't drive them out.

Drive them out, Aftab. Drive them far away – and then I'll come home. I want to come home.

Your friend,
Laxman Kachru

P.S. I've just read through what I've written. It sounds like a bhashan and I'm sorry for that. But mere dost, that's how I really feel. I miss you, I miss home and I had to write down these thoughts before I lose my faith in them.

L.K.

P.P.S. Thank you for listening, and understanding, I feel as if I've just got my voice back. Suddenly I feel, maybe we'll meet again soon.

Your friend
L.K.

Aftab read and re-read the letter many times. He didn't know what to make of it. He crumpled it, threw it away, but then went and fetched it back, smoothening out the creases — reading and re-reading. He didn't know how to feel. Suddenly, his mind was clouded with doubts. And he couldn't tell right from wrong. For the first time since it all began, he started to wonder which side he should be on.

15

Deeper and deeper into the
blackening

'Akram, AKRAM – AK-RAM – BHH-AI!!' searching, searching, searching, deeper and deeper into the blackening.

'Akram Bhai,' cold, shivering, water everywhere, drowning.

'Akram,' a whisper.

'Akram,' a prayer.

'Who is Akram?'

Suddenly wide awake, widely wildly awake.

'Who is Akram?'

Who's Akram!'

'Who's Akram?'

'Who is Akram ….'

A lash, stinging, across his already raw face.

'Who is Akram?'

Silence – crack – another jarring blow.

'Who is Akram?'

He tried to see, but it was blinding – had he become blind? Whose voice was this? What was the source of this pain?

'Who is Akram?'

The teeth, the few left in his mouth, were already loose, becoming looser with every blow.

'Who is Akram?'

'Akram – Bhai,'

Who is Akram Bhai?'

'My bhai – my brother.'

'Where is he?'

Shake of already shaking head. Blow. Where? Shake. He honestly didn't know. This was just why Akram Bhai had never told him.

'Where?'

'Home.'

'Where is home?'

'Very far away.' 'Where?' 'Across cold mountains, many weeks journey.'

'Akram is here with you in India.'

'No!'

Another blow. Another tooth. Gone.

'Where is Akram?'

It went on like that for hours, days … weeks?

Disoriented, Feroze had no idea of time anymore. Only the fire in those green eyes that had saved him once kept him going now. He tried hard to banish the name from inside himself. But it was too much a part of him now. It was too much to part with. If he gave it up, he would give up his life.

'Is Akram the name of the firangi we killed up in the hills? Is it him?'

Feroze's eyes fluttered open again. 'No … .' It cannot be, he mouthed. They pulled him up, walked him out, telling him he must identify the body. 'This is the man who was hanging around, looking at you and the boy being arrested. You must identify him.'

As they brought him out of the interrogation cell, Major Ramneeq was almost horrified at what they had done to him. He turned his face, trying in disgust to wipe out the sympathy which arose unbidden and unwanted in his chest. When he looked up again, it was at an old, shivering man, draped on the shoulders of jawans. Unable to take a step unaided. Interrogation had to be brutal, but, he reminded himself, so were the methods of these brutalized militants.

The body that lay under the sheet was white, drained of blood and life. Feroze held his breath. He was nauseous. The sheet was being pulled off. But he didn't want to look – he couldn't. If it were his brother, his soul, his heart would break. He couldn't.

He was forced to. Look. White, ashen-faced, the look of horror not yet gone from the hollowed cheeks. Feroze held his face impassive, expressionless, but inside, his heart was joyous. Oh, this was Akram alright. Akram Bhai's work. But not, thank god, his body.

For there, in the cold light of the mortuary, lay Sajid. Their former friend, boss – now their enemy. Well, no longer their enemy – he was gone now. Without needing any facts, Feroze could imagine what had happened. They would have been after Akram – the army guys – the shepherds and the dog. They may even have shot at Bhai, but then, once again, Bhai had outwitted them. Somehow, he'd got hold of Sajid, as he'd always wanted to and let his pursuers believe that they had killed him. This was just like him -- the bravest, most cunning of them all. But he held his face expressionless until they asked, 'Is this Akram?'

And then he broke down and yelled and wept. Like an orphaned child. 'Akram, mere Akram Bhai.'

And try as they might, they couldn't stem his tears or silence his sobs. Finally when they took him back to his cell, he slept. More soundly than he had since Akram Bhai had first disappeared.

And Akram? After emerging from the heart of the frigid pool, pocketing the hollow reed that gave him life-giving air, he made for the cave that was home now. But then, he had come face to face with Sajid. He was on the run too, thinking it was him they were after. The two former allies faced each other, stopped in their tracks for a moment. Each one thinking how much the other had grown, hardened. The younger man took in the fading glory of the older man and didn't return the greeting. Instead, he shot him, once, twice. Dead. Cold within minutes. Then dug into his own wound and mingled his blood with that of the dead man's. That would keep the tracking dog busy, at least for a while.

And he'd made good his escape. Again.

16

'No!'

Aftab's heart was pounding. This was the moment he'd always lived for. To be with Akram Bhai. Up in the woods, in hiding. Now he'd be given instructions, be told what to do. Now he was going to prove that he was like the beetle that had made its way through the window mesh, so long ago. Unlike the others that had banged impotently on the wire mesh. He was ready for action. And, if necessary, he'd burn himself on the flame. Like that beetle had. He'd go out shouting the glory of the name of Akram Bhai.

He followed, almost unseeing, as Shazia whispered through the thickening night forest. So carried away in his thoughts was he that he stopped short as he came to the mouth of the musky cave, suddenly wondering where he was and how he got here. Shazia had already gone in. He was overcome with shyness. Aapa's new role in their group embarrassed him, now that he was going to see them together for the first time. He hesitated, heard her giggle, then walked in, to see his sister in Akram Bhai's arms.

'Ah Aftab, my hero, come, come into my arms, my brother ...,' he held out his arms, still sitting with his leg bound and stretched before him. Aftab looked down, scuffing his toes against the stone.

'Arre Shazia, are you my bride, or is he?' Akram laughed, 'See how he blushes and hesitates like a girl about to be married!'

Aftab could have died of embarrassment; he was completely tongue-tied, frozen. 'Come on, silly – aiee, Boey,' Shazia prodded him.

Then he was in Akram's embrace. His heart bursting. 'You're alright, Akram Bhai?' he said, as soon as he could manage.

'Yes,' he smiled, 'I am alright, they can't get rid of Akram's Kashmir Action Group that easily.'

'They'll never get rid of you, Bhai, no one can do that. I was so worried, the ... the Major said that they'd killed you.'

'Yes, I know, your sister told me, she's been my lifeline, you know.' They both watched as she produced fresh medicines and bandages from her phiran. 'Ao, little brother, now you're my brother-in-law, huh, now that you know?'

'It was a well-kept secret by both of you, I'd never have guessed.'

As they settled down to their kahwas, the mood changed. It was time to get down to serious business. They had urgent and important work to do.

'First, about Feroze.'

'It was horrible, Bhai, he was already shaking very, very badly, even, even before. And then, the cries from the room where he was,' he couldn't go on. The images of blood conjured up again.

'Yes, it is as I feared. He cannot take more torture now, I think we all know this. I'm in no condition for another daring raid.'

'He's too well-guarded, Akram,' Shazia added.

'Ah, guards can always be swayed, one way or another. But yes, you're right. In the current mahaul, I do think an escape attempt would be foolhardy.'

'Then what? We can't leave him there. Let me try, Akram Bhai.' Aftab leaned forward, waiting for instructions, ready for action. At last.

'No, they're watching you, they'll know you'll make some attempt. Besides, you cannot. You're too young.'

Aftab was crushed. So, he was still the bacha, too little for big tasks.

'But I have a plan. Shazia, meri jaan. It's you who will have to do this.'

'Gladly,' she clasped his hand to her heart, 'Just tell me what to do.'

'It's you who'll have to "persuade" one of the guards.'

'How can she?'

'She's a woman and a beautiful one,' a pause for an endearing, persuasive smile, 'She has a woman's weapons, no one can say no.'

'NO!'

'No?'

Aftab was standing, swaying as the full meaning of Akram's intentions became clear. Akram's eyes hardened, it seemed that the cave became a few degrees colder.

'No – I'll not allow it.'

'You won't allow my instructions to be carried out?'

'No – No – I'll not allow her to do something like that, she's my sister.'

'Yes – and my wife – don't forget that.'

'It's you who seems to have forgotten – how can you expect your wife to …?' Aftab was shaking, his voice edgy with anger. He'd never stood up to Akram Bhai like this, never spoken in this voice. But this, this was preposterous.

The air became darker, colder as did Akram's voice – there was ice in it as in his eyes. 'Little brother, control yourself and mind how you speak in front of my wife ….'

'But ….'

'Silence!'

And there was.

Shazia stood up and went to her brother, trying to calm him down, not sure if she could calm him at all, but knowing she couldn't even start to try with the other. She herself was shocked by this suggestion, but not had the heart to say anything. Akram had decided, it was the only way, 'Boey, don't ....'

Aftab shook her off, 'No, no, no. This I cannot agree to. Her being with you, well, that's one thing. But using her to get through the jail guard – that's, that's just – horrible.'

'Aftab, alright, alright, sit down.' His voice was stiller now.

'No.'

'I agree – what I suggested was horrible. Now sit down.'

'You agree?'

'Yes.'

'With me?' This was something new.

'Yes, yes – now sit down I said, I can't look at you away in the shadows.'

They both came back to him. Sat on either side of the man they loved, but the man who had just made this terrible suggestion. He took each of their hands in his.

'Yes, it's horrible, unthinkable, undoable. Yes, I wouldn't agree to it myself, at any price.'

He waited then went on, 'Except ...,' he felt Aftab's hand about to pull away, felt Shazia's soft one tense. His voice became soft, soothing. Hypnotic. 'Except that when I think of poor Feroze, my heart breaks and my mind can't think straight. He's being beaten, tortured, brutalized. Probably, even as we speak, they are draining the blood out of him.' Akram watched the boy flinch at the image of blood. He had known he would need this weakness sometime and now, the time was here. 'When I close my eyes, all I can see is blood – Feroze's blood. Blood running like tears from his wounded body. And my own tears are blood too. He was barely surviving after I'd left to hide in these mountains,' he watched Aftab, who knew that he was right. 'But now ...,' he let the images sink in, 'I wish he were dead.'

'How can you say that?'

'Then what? Aftab mia, you'd have him go on languishing in a lock-up, is it? You'd have them break his bones one by one, pull out his teeth, his hair – you'd give them the pleasure of seeing his blood spill day after pain-washed day? You'd have his shaking become so bad that he'd be reduced to a vegetable – you'd have that?' His voice was soft, softly cruel. He saw the boy conjure up the image. He waited, let the picture weaken him. Then moved in further.

'Don't forget, he could have got you into trouble. A lot of trouble. But he held his tongue. At great cost to himself. At the cost of his blood, his life. He saved you with the ultimate sacrifice. You cannot do this much for him?'

The silence was dense, a living thing. Moments went by. Blood and pain swam before them. Then Shazia sighed, 'What do I have to do?'

This time Aftab's hand went slack in the older man's. Akram had won. *Again*.

He went on to explain, in his soft, beautiful voice that the word 'prostitute' would not apply here. Shazia would be a martyr to 'the cause'. The flame that she was would glow higher, brighter – would not be diminished at all. And while he spoke, Aftab's heart became heavier and Shazia's fluttered with horror at the thought of what she must do. But no one challenged the older man again.

And so the plan was made, the trap set and Feroze's fate sealed.

They left separately, Aftab first, under the cover of deep night. Slinking unseen although a guard stood across the street from their door.

He lay awake till Shazia slipped in. She pressed a kiss on her brother's forehead and he smelt the presence of Akram about her. He turned over, letting the tears flow now.

There would be more to flow.

17

And it was done ...

Major Ramneeq was edgy. It was too quiet. Far too quiet. And this fellow they'd caught, he wouldn't give them anything. No matter how hard they tried. No matter how hard they hit. A search had revealed that this was not his first stint in army confinement. He'd been rescued from a jail in a daring raid which had left several jawans maimed and dead.

So he was a veteran. All they'd got from him was the fact that this Akram fellow was dead. He had been killed in the chase up on the hills. He seemed to have been a leader. But the captive would give no more, neither a name for himself, nor his outfit. Nor would the boy. Aftab stuck resolutely to his story of the threat to his sister. The only change he'd made was that since he couldn't come up with enough money, he'd managed, instead, to have them agree that he would look after the near-crippled militant who hadn't been able to keep up with the others when they'd made good their escape.

What troubled him was that he hadn't come up with this explanation the first day, even though he was pressed, threatened and cajoled. They'd had to let the boy go home after his trauma and injury. When he returned for questioning the next day, he came up with this theory quite readily. There could be three explanations for this. One, that it was the simple truth, that he'd been too traumatized to tell them the first day. The second that he'd thought it up later, to cover up actual truths. The third, and most disturbing, was that he'd been tutored by someone to say this. Disturbing, because he had not been out of the house, nor had anyone, except his friend, Angad, been in to see him. Did it mean that more members of the family were involved?

The Major shut his eyes, weary. He was a man of action. This sleuthing business, especially where young children were involved, was hard on him. Not that he'd want to give it up to any one else. Just. Just …. He looked around, made sure he was alone and then wrapped his arms across his chest, almost hugging himself. Hugging the emptiness of the air around him. The space that should have been filled by his son. His forever faraway son. He never thought, when he'd lost his son in that courtroom, that that would be the hardest battle of his life. The one battle where there were no victors.

'Ah! I'm becoming an old softie, aren't I?' he thought ruefully to himself. These boys had no idea of the price he was paying for their adventures.

And why was it all so quiet? Why were none of them making any move? This inaction and waiting were beginning to tell on his nerves. He would finish this case and apply for leave. Yes, he'd take leave and go and meet his wife – ex-wife and in-laws. He would try to come to some compromise. He was willing for any compromise. Now. They'd have to see that he couldn't survive without his son. After all, they were maybe his ex-wife and ex-in-laws, but the child was not his ex-son! He'd always be his son. 'And I'll always be his father!'

The thought cheered him up. His orderly was glad to see the smile on his saab's lips that had been too long set in grim, straight lines.

Night fell. And all was dark and quiet. As it should be. Except that nothing was going to be as it should be again. Shazia crept into the room. 'I'm going,' she whispered into her brother's ear.

'Wait, I'll go with you.'

'Shh! No, leave it, I don't want you there.'

'Akram would ... .'

'No! He forbade and I forbid it too.'

'Aapa ...,' a little boy appeal, a last ditch attempt to put off the awful inevitable.

'Stay!' Her voice was a whispered command. She held the flat of her palm open. As though commanding a dog. 'Stay.' Then softer, 'It's alright, it'll be over by morning.'

'You may need help.'

'I'll manage – my prayers are with me.'

'As are mine. You have all you need?'

She indicated the little bundle under her arm and was gone. And Aftab was left alone. Knives turning in his belly as helpless rage simmered.

High up in the dark cave, Akram too bit down on his tongue. He'd never felt so helpless before and it enraged him, engulfed him now.

She watched from the shadows. She consulted Akram's map. A dog barked. She stiffened. Waited. She was not patient by nature, but knew that impatience now was a foe, patience a friend. She waited. Until one of the guards was alone ..... He heard a tinkle of bangles. An unfamiliar sound nowadays. The sound held a question, a promise. The sentry held his breath. A little girl giggle and the tinkle of glass on glass again. 'Kaun?'

'Shhh.'

He was about to shout to his partner, raise an alarm.

'Hush!' a pretty voice, beguiling. 'Hush – why call others who may spoil the fun?'

'What?'

Oh no, had she picked a wrong one, one with morals, ethics?

'Shhh! Softly, why share what you can have all by yourself? I've been watching you, waiting for that ugly friend of yours to leave us alone. Just you and I.'

She showed herself then. Dressed in trinkets and a green kurta that echoed her emerald eyes. Eyes that held promise. He hesitated, torn between duty and desire. The latter won.

'How much?'

'Huh!' the indignation was only partly pretended. 'Just forget it. Do I look like a common call girl to you – I chose you, don't you understand?'

He looked. No – what he saw was indeed not a common call girl – but just a girl. A beautiful one, at that.

'Then what?'

'I want a few minutes with the prisoner.'

'No.'

'Let me explain.' She beckoned him into the shadows. 'Lest we are caught. You see, Bhai Sahib,' and she filled her eyes with tears, letting them hang prettily on her dark lashes. 'You see, we are betrothed, your prisoner and I. We've been promised to each other for years. We were to marry next month. I know that he is breaking now. I know that he has not long to live ...,' her tear-filled voice brought him closer, he inhaled her musky perfume and was torn between sympathy and lust. 'He's in a bad way, is he not?'

He nodded. For he'd seen the prisoner himself just this morning. He looked like an old, feeble man, not one to be married to this beautiful young woman.

'Sahib,' she said, gracefully dropping the 'bhai' part of the address, 'Would you have him die, leaving me a widow before I'm even married?' The tears spilled. He baulked. 'No, no, I cannot help him escape. That would be suicide for me.'

'Of course not,' she took his hands in her soft little ones, 'I'd not expect so much from you. I only want to meet him once. To give him a little food I have cooked. To bid him good-bye and request him to release me from the engagement. Then I won't be a widow, will I – will I?'

The tears spilled. And as she had hoped, he sprang up to dry them.

'Don't cry – er – er ….'

'Fawzia,'

'Fawzia Begum, don't cry. It'll be alright.'

And it was done.

Feeling filthy, still shuddering, she was quietly slipped into Feroze's cell.

'Shazia, how?'

'Don't ask,' was all she could manage before she buried her head into his bony shoulder and cried her heart out. Then she looked at him and cried some more, for he was a shadow, a skeleton – only the shaking of the limbs confirmed that he was indeed Feroze, and he was still alive. She looked into his eyes, wise beyond their years. He looked into hers and knew at once how she had got here.

'Who told you to do this? Who put you up to this? It can't be Akram Bhai, he would never … .'

'Let it be. We have no time. I have a message – Akram lives.'

'Yah Allah! I had a feeling … so, it was Sajid they found and thought it was Bhai?'

'Yes, you did well. Akram will be pleased that you understood.'

'Shazia – beware of Javed and Imran – they've gone over to the other side.'

'I'll tell him – forget it, they were a burden anyway, Akram said.'

'Yes, Aftab's a good boy though. Shazia – how is Akram Bhai?'

'He is hurt, but recovering. He …,' she uncovered the box of halwa, Feroze's favourite sweet. 'He sent this, he said you'd understand.' They looked at each other, she touched his hand. 'He said that he was sorry.'

Feroze collapsed on his bunk. So, this was it. His time had come. Was he ready? He wasn't sure.

But one thing he was sure of was that he couldn't take the beating, the torture, the questioning anymore. He knew that it would kill him.

He looked at the sweets, he looked at Shazia's lovely, anxious face. She had gone through so much to bring this release to him. Akram Bhai must have suffered so much sending her like this. Sending him this sweetest poison.

He took a handful and chewed it with toothless gums. He nodded, smiled. Yes it was better to die at Akram Bhai's hand, rather than give the enemy satisfaction.

The sentry was back by the time the second handful was gone. He indicated that time was running out.

Feroze leaned forward and kissed the girl's forehead. 'Peace be with you. Give my best to your brother and husband. Tell Akram Bhai I'll wait for him in jannat but not to hurry there. Tell him I love him, I'll never forget all the debts I owe him. Tell him ... .'

'Fawzia Begum – now.' The door rattled,

'The cause lives on, Feroze Bhai ... Khuda hafiz,' and she was gone.

So was he.

18

Death hung too close that day

The newspapers bannered two headlines that day. 'Terrorist Akram of Kashmir Action Group killed in Encounter' said one. 'Death in Custody' said the other.

Although they knew the truth and facts behind the stories, Shazia and Aftab couldn't help but pour over and read and re-read every word. And feel relief at one and deep sorrow at the other. Shazia, especially, was wracked with guilt. She couldn't get over the fact that Feroze Bhai had, in fact, died by her hands. However necessary it had been, it was she who had delivered death to him. Aftab saw her looking at her hands and went up to her, filled her hands with his own. He knew what was going on in her mind, but, as always, he didn't have the words to console her.

Their father was reading the paper out to his wife. 'Good – I'm so glad – I hope they all die!' was her comment. Abbu grunted, 'When will the day come when we read the paper and there are no deaths reported?' A collective sadness shadowed the room. Death hung too close that day.

Death hung too close that day. Major Ramneeq examined the preliminary report by the doctor. The beating, alright, the torture had been hard. Yes. But none of the wounds inflicted had been fatal. Not that the human rights' people would have any of that. They'd hang on to the fact that he was a sick man, ailing. That he'd been denied 'adequate medical attention ....'

These people, they had no idea what the army was up against. It was easy to feel that they should be good and kind and everyone should have their every right intact. But how do you deal with the demons who brutalized others? How was the army to protect the innocent without extracting vital information from these militants, by any means possible? It made Ramneeq's blood boil. He was supposed to be preparing for the arrival of the Human Rights Commission people, but he couldn't help thinking what a waste of time it was going to be. There was so much to do – he needed to follow up with this boy, Aftab, and now was as good a time as any. He should be trying to squeeze more out of Angad. Instead, here he was ....

There was a knock on the door. Captain Suraj stood there. 'Sir, the post-mortem report on the killed militant, the one identified as Akram.'

'Yes, Suraj – what does it say?'

'Sir, it's strange, sir. The bullets that killed him – they were not our bullets. Sir, the man, whoever it is, was killed by someone else.'

Major Ramneeq held his hand out for the report. 'There's more, sir – the reason why the dog confirmed that the body was the one whose blood trail we were following. The blood in the wound, sir – there were two blood types. One belonging to the body. And another one – probably the militant we had shot.'

'Wily fox!' snapped Ramneeq, opening the file. Where would this new information lead them to now? He looked at the photograph of the dead man. He'd have the photo taken to the halwai and the young lad who worked there. Was this the man with young Aftab in the shop? Or not?

As it turned out, it wasn't. The face cut was similar. The hair was shorter. But no, both the halwai and the boy confirmed that the dead man was not the one who had sat in their shop with Aftab.

Another post-mortem later, and the world was upside down. Feroze, the custody death, had indeed not died from wounds. He had been poisoned. Poisoned? There was halwa found in his viscera. Sweet mixed with poison. Where did it come from? And who could have brought it to him in the prison?

After being literally interrogated by the Human Rights walas – interrogated as though he was the criminal here – Major Ramneeq was in a furious mood.

He lined up all the guards, sentries, jawans who had been on duty the night before. Who had been where, what were they doing? They must account for every minute of their duty period. And then account for their off-duty activities. Quaking, each one gave a full account of his whereabouts. They'd never seen their boss this angry. He was a good man – always concerned for their welfare, rarely expecting anything in return. The questioning was intensive. It was like squeezing water from a dry rock.

At last, exhausted and spent, Ramneeq called off the interrogation. Dismissed everyone and went home. He didn't feel well at all. When a hesitant knock sounded on the door, all he could do was to sit up in his chair and ask whoever it was to come in. It was one of his men. Laxmi Narain, who had been on duty that night. He was anxious and glanced perpetually behind him. He bore a heavy secret.

'Go on, Laxmi.'

'Sir, forgive me sir, and may the heavens strike me down if my suspicions are wrong, sir. Sir, you understand, they're suspicions only, sir?'

Ramneeq drew in a deep, deep breath. His patience was wearing out, but he knew he'd have to let the jawan unburden himself, justify himself before he could, would reveal what he'd come for.

'Sir, I hope you know that I'd cut off my tongue before saying something like this about a colleague, but sir, seeing you angry today sir, seeing how those

Dilliwalas were harassing you sir. Sir, you've been so good to me sir ….'

'Alright, Laxmi, get on with it, out with it. What do you know?'

'I – I'm not sure sir, it's not as if I saw with my own eyes, sir. But sir ….'

'Go on.'

'Sir, early this morning – Kumar sir.'

'Hawaldar Kumar?'

'Yes, sir, sir before I take names, before I point fingers, sir, I hope ….'

'What you say will remain between us, Laxmi – I will ensure that nothing is traced back to you.'

'Thank you sir, that's all I wanted.'

'So, what about Kumar, what happened this morning?'

'He was bragging, sir. Showing off that he had been with a woman in here. He said he could bring her here any time he wanted. He quietly told a couple of us that he could bring her for us, if we wanted. I got angry with him sir, by god, very angry. I told him that it was against the rules. Reminded him that he was a married man … I told him I'd never ….'

'And what has this to do with the poisoning of the prisoner?'

'I don't know sir. It's only a suspicion. He didn't say anything more. But sir, she was probably the only outsider in the Cantt. I don't know ….'

'Did he say anything else about the woman – describe her, in any way?'

Laxmi looked away, thoroughly embarrassed, hanging his head, examining his neatly polished shoes, he whispered, 'He said sir, that she was very young. Said she was a hoor-ki-pari – beautiful as an angel – with eyes the colour of the greenest pannas.'

Shazia's young face, her emerald eyes sprang into the Major's consciousness unbidden, unwanted. No – surely not – yet ...? He needed to think. He thanked Laxmi Narain, praised him for his alertness, righteousness and loyalty. But he had to listen to more justification before he could finally get rid of him.

Although tired, Ramneeq's mind was alert, racing backwards and forwards to his encounters with Aftab. And his sister. Of course it was a wild assumption. A hunch, at best. A story full of loopholes. So it may be just a red herring and lead to nothing. There were many beautiful Kashmiri girls with the prettiest green eyes. Shazia was one of hundreds, probably.

And yet, the nagging suspicion wouldn't go away. And the Major had learned, long ago, to trust his instincts. He recalled his earlier suspicion about Aftab. How, sometimes, he'd be completely tongue-tied, at a loss for words. Then he'd go off home and when questioned again, he'd have the words, the explanations rolling, almost glibly off his tongue. This was not the first time that he'd felt that boy was being tutored. Could that tutor possibly be his sister – the emerald-eyed Shazia?

19

And as always, she believed

The restlessness grew in Shazia like a live thing. She could barely tolerate her mother's exhortations to involve her in household chores. She desperately wanted to go to be with Akram. And yet, strangely, she felt she also needed to be away from him. Away from it all – the hiding, the secrecy. The danger. She rubbed warm mustard oil into Amir's head, his chatter soothed her a little. He talked of merry things. Even when he sought her advice over things that troubled him, they seemed such happy things, compared to the life-altering, earth-shattering, murdering problems she'd had to deal with of late.

Finally, her tasks were almost over. She couldn't wait anymore. She called to Aftab, told him she needed to go, and asked him to finish the remaining chores for her. He agreed gladly. She smiled at him and whispered,

'Gladly – for me or for Akram?' It delighted her that she could embarrass him quite so easily!

But she couldn't find Akram; he wasn't where he should have been. Where on earth could he be – and with that leg of his? She waited in the cave, lying on his bedding, smelling the smell of him, turning over the torn paper with curt instructions:

11.30 tonight Aftab ALONE

Finally, the emptiness of the place filled her to a breaking point. She left. Wandered over the hills. But Akram's need for action had infected her as well. She wandered down to the market. She found Angad there, tucking into samosas. Ah! Here was something to do, at last.

'Always hungry, huh, Chottey Boey?' she gave the boy a playful whack on his stomach.

'Ow! Oh, Shazia Aapa, sorry,' he spluttered, 'Here have some?' but the fried smell made her nauseous. 'Will you walk with me?'

He walked with her, so proud to be by her side. He glanced at her from under his dense lashes, and then away to see who was watching him walk with this beautiful woman.

'So Angad Bhai, you've been talking to my brother – what else has he revealed? Anything I should know?'

'Nothing much Aapa – though believe me, I've tried. But he's very quiet and secretive about where he's been. Also, Aapa ...,' he hesitated and was prodded on by her encouraging smile, 'Aapa, although he claims he hasn't, I think he's really been exercising. Have you noticed his muscles recently?' She laughed, 'No.'

'No, really, Aapa. I noticed first when he came back after a long time to play cricket with us. Wow, he was running like – like a man and his shirt barely closed over his chest and arms. Not like us boys. Then, then Aapa, when he got hurt, at the playground, remember?'

How could she forget?

'He was dizzy, so I tried to carry him, but he was too heavy. I thought he was becoming a motu. But later, in the jeep, gosh, Aapa, you should have seen his muscles jumping!'

'It happens to all you boys, Angu, there's nothing special, it's just a part of growing up.'

'I'm not so sure, Aapa – not those kind of muscles.'

'So what do you make of it, Angad?'

His voice dropped to a conspiratorial whisper, he was in full flow now, 'Aapa – I think he's been in training. He's being trained somewhere.'

'Where?'

'I – I'm not sure, but Aapa, these days you can't be sure of anything. My papa says the militants have got to the best families, the best boys. My papa says that it's our duty to help the armed forces.'

'And what do you say?'

'Aapa – he's your brother and my best friend. I'd thought that I would talk to him, convince him to mend his ways, forget about these jungly militants and dangerous games. But Aapa – he just won't listen, hai na? He won't even let me start talking to him about all this. He just shuts me up.'

'Hmm – so?'

'So, Aapa, I don't know yet, I haven't decided, but sometimes I feel it may be best to tell the Major saab everything. See, Aapa, he, I mean Afti, was holding that fellow's hand in the jeep – trying to help him because the man was so frightened, he was shaking like a little baby about to do susu!!' Angad laughed, then instantly sobered up as he saw the grim, anxious look in her eyes. How stupid could he be?

Major Ramneeq was on his way to the market. He needed nothing more than a walk. But he got more than that. For there was Shazia, standing, talking, with Angad. They were an odd couple to see together – or were they? A sense of urgency filled him – he must get to the truth of this before the inevitable happened.

She turned to look at Angad. She stared deep into his eyes. And he was pinned. She stood silent, skipping a few heartbeats. Trying to assess what to do. For she saw before her the sweet, chubby-faced, flame-cheeked boy with merry eyes who had stood by his friend, her brother. A little boy who would be a man in some years. A good man, a loyal friend. She tried to see him through Akram's eyes. A threat. But try as she might, she couldn't see him as one. A threat to Aftab, to her – to Akram.

'Wait,' she said to him. A soft appeal. 'Before you go to report him – wait. I'll try to talk to him again –

warn him of dangers. He'll come around to our way of thinking – yours and mine. But I need time – will you give it to me?' she appealed.

And of course, he would. He said, 'But only a few days Aapa. I don't think we should wait endlessly. There could be real danger. To innocent people. To us. To him.'

She had to be satisfied with that. She left him standing there and walked away, deep in troubled thought. There wasn't much time. Again, she had the sensation of time slipping from her fingers. And she seemed unable to stop it. She'd have to tell Akram about this, of course.

And, of course, she knew what he'd say. 'There are no friends, Shazia. An enemy is almost always an enemy, but a friend can sometimes become a foe. No one is above suspicion and you must never forget that. If, in this path that you and I have chosen, there is a threat, even a perceived threat, then it must be eliminated. Silenced. Leaving no room for doubt.'

And of course, he was right. But still: the merry eyes, the baby face. The sweet childhood friend. But Akram would have to be told.

And she did. She gave Aftab the message about his meeting with Akram later tonight. Alone. She left, pretending to go to the market, but not without Ammi watching her with suspicious eyes and muttering reproachfully about the restlessness of girls nowadays. Aftab was quick to go sit by her and distract her by rubbing oil onto her tired feet and nodding knowingly as she prattled on about finding a suitable match for her daughter before it was too late.

Akram was in such a state of agitation that she didn't dare scold him for not being there earlier. The blood in her veins turned to ice as he told her that now it wasn't just the army he had to be wary of, but Sajid's men. They were after him to avenge the death of their leader. 'And do you know who was with them – on the look-out for me? Javed and Imran – those gaddaars, after all I've taught them. I swear, I'll kill them before they touch a hair of my head.'

She calmed him a little, but instead he turned morose. 'Shazia tell your little brother to take utmost caution. Javed and Imran are not above anything.'

'Akram … don't, don't let him come to any danger. He's only just a child. If, if something needs to be done, let me ….'

'Ah Shazia, no, not that again. You know, or you should, by now, that I would never endanger the child, he's my brother too, you forget.'

'It's not that I forget, it's just …,' but he assured her that there was nothing he would do to harm the boy. *And as always, she believed.*

She wished she didn't have to bring up another uncomfortable issue to discuss. She wished that today their talk would be about their love, their romance. The house they would build. The children they would have together. She sighed.

'What is it, my love?' he smiled, 'I'm sorry, I've been so involved in my troubles, I've failed to notice that there are some of your own. Tell me – what is it?' So she told him about the danger Angad posed. Told him that he'd allowed her a few days, but then had sworn to go to the army.

'It's inevitable,' he said when she'd finished, 'it was always going to happen. I will explain it to Aftab what needs to be done.'

'No!' she said, alarmed. She knew her brother. Such a thing would be unthinkable for him. Impossible. 'No, I'll do whatever needs to be done. You must leave him out of this.'

'You, my darling, have done enough. More than your fair share. I will not make things difficult for my little brother-in-law. If necessary, I'll do it myself – alright?' Of course, he persuaded her. *He always could.*

It was getting dark outside. She couldn't stay out much longer. There was no time to linger, no time to love. A hurried embrace was all that they managed.

'Till next time,' he promised.

'Till next time,' she agreed and whispered Inshahallah as she left him. Feeling, as always, that she was leaving a part of herself in that high, hidden animal cave. There was the other thing she'd wanted to tell him, share with him today. But later, now. Not today. Today, he had enough on his mind.

20

Akram had caught his fish

Under cover of the dark, dark night, Aftab steals away. He is proud of himself at this moment. For this is the moment he has lived for these past years, since he joined Akram and Feroze Bhai.

The night, the darkness leaps up at him as he enters the forest. His courage sways a little. He dreads the solitude. He takes a deep breath and starts to hum a tune. Then shuts himself up quickly. How stupid can he be. He must be soundless. Like Akram has always taught him to be. He tries to think of this or that, but nothing can distract him from the dark that fills the space around and presses into his eyes as if to blind him. The sharp smell of pine, the grating of cicadas. The high wind hushing the trees, whispering secrets, cracking of twigs, all add up to the feeling, 'I'm alone.'

Akram – Akram Bhai. Now there's a thought he can focus on. As he clambers forward, his mind meanders backward. To the beginning. When he first met his Akram Bhai.

It was a beautiful sun-ripened morning. But Aftab was on his own. He'd not done his homework. So he'd skipped school. Of course, his father, a schoolteacher in the same school, would get to know. He would feel the lash of his father's tongue and, later, the stick. But that was later. For now, he was completely happy, diving into the gentle Jhelum. Swimming out to its soft centre and lying in wait … . Then he had it. Clutched firmly in his hand, held aloft. The silver fish thrashed, but his fingers did not let go. That's when he saw the man sitting on the bank, watching him. He smiled, waved and Aftab waved back.

'That's very impressive,' the man said, looking at the fish as Aftab waded to the shallows. 'Can you do it again?' There was the faintest hint of challenge in his voice. Aftab handed the fish over to the stranger, dived back again to his spot. Then waited, making himself a block of wood in his stillness. Then, quicker than the eye could follow, the man saw the boy disappear under the shimmering water and come up with a whoop of delight, the fish flaying in his triumphant hands. The stranger asked him how he did it and Aftab, flushed with recent victory, feeling most important, gave the stranger a step-by-step lesson on patience, watchfulness, stillness and speed. By the end of the lecture, Akram's eyes were ablaze. He'd asked the boy about himself and the child, enjoying the company of this handsome man, flattered by the attention, told him all about his family, his likes, dislikes. And also, that he was often bored.

And Akram needed to hear just that. He'd caught his fish too.

Of course, that's not how Aftab remembered all of it. It was as if there'd been an empty space in his life. And now, it was filled by Akram who showed him the most amazing weapons, gave him money whenever he needed it and most of all, brought excitement into the life that had been dull till now.

The hoot of a large owl frightens Aftab out of his thoughts. Animals whisper to him. His ears are filled with slithery, hissy sounds. Is it his imagination or is it a snake that shadows past him? In spite of his determination, inspite of his feeling of great pride that he has been summoned, he just feels alone. Inspite of the best intentions, he longs to be with someone. He now wishes that he had Shazia with him. And then is immediately ashamed of wanting a girl-woman's protection. But then, again, he longs for home. Right now, he wouldn't mind ousting Amir out from the comfort of lying between Abbu and Ammi. No matter how much he chides his weak heart, it fails him. The wind up here is higher, wilder – as untamed as the terrain. Then he sees it. The tiniest flash. Then it's gone. He watches, breath held. There it is again. Off and on. On and off. Enemy or friend? Friend or enemy? He does not know. He steps behind a tall deodar – bare and wounded by lightening, but still sturdy. He watches. The light flashes closer. The 'plop' of the night jar.

Akram? He knows that Bhai can imitate this bird perfectly. There it is again. 'Plop', from the darkness. Aftab tries to return the call. It isn't right it comes out clumsy. But he hears a soft laugh. He knows this laugh. He is home.

'I'm sorry, my brother,' Akram Bhai wraps comforting arms around him. 'I'm sorry, it was hard – and very frightening, no?'

'No, no,' assures Aftab, 'Of course not – I could do it a thousand times over,' and shyly, 'For you.'

'For me or for my wife?' he teases just like Shazia.

'For the cause,' says the boy.

'Shabash – that's my soldier.'

The kahwa is bitter, the bakarkhani stale and dry. But it is the sweetest meal that Aftab has ever eaten. When he offers to help with the cleaning up, Akram laughs, 'I knew you'd not like to see me doing a woman's work.'

'How is the wound on your leg now, Akram Bhai?' He's brought some of the sarson oil, stolen from his mother's kitchen, and rubs it now into his feet, hard as the stones they walk on. And as unrelenting.

'I'll live,' says Akram. *And who was to know then that his casual reply would become a lie. So soon.*

It's time to take leave. Akram hugs the boy and is happy to see that his arms and chest are solid, he has kept up with his exercise. He is in active training. The stage is set. The plan unfolded. The tears for those who must go have dried and hardened under Akram's clever persuasion. He is a master of persuasion.

'And again, Chottey Bhai – not a word of this to your Aapa. However much she may pretend otherwise, she has a woman's heart. And you – a man to the world now – are still a baby brother to her.'

'Yes, Akram Bhai,' the child, trying so hard to be a man, assents. Then again, to reassure himself, 'And you say there will be time enough for me to get away, no, Akram Bhai?'

'Yes, yes Aftab, yes. Press down the button, pull the drawstring and get out of there. And don't look back. That's all. There'll be enough time for you.'

'Okay, Bhai,' in the voice of a frightened child.

'You are ready, aren't you, Aftab? I'm not mistakenly placing my faith and trust in a whimpering child, am I?'

'No sir – no. I will do what you ask of me. You will be proud of me.'

'I know I will.'

Now flush with burgeoning confidence, 'The next time we meet, Akram Bhai, your "shabash" will be for something truly worthwhile.'

'Yes – I know,' whispers the man.

For he knows, that for the child, there will be no next time. And in spite of himself, his training, he is sorry.

'Go, my brave soldier. You alone, can make the name of the Kashmir Action Group shine for eternity.'

After the boy is gone, Akram lies down on his mat, emptied, drained. This, he knows, is the end of his little outfit. For now. Javed and Imran have defected. Feroze is dead. Aftab will soon be a martyr. And Shazia may never forgive her husband for the loss of her beloved brother.

He is spent. He cannot think anymore right now. He will start afresh, begin with another recruitment drive. Again. Tomorrow. All of that, tomorrow. For now, he sleeps.

And he doesn't, for once, hear the approach of stealthy footsteps ... .

21

He hadn't thought there'd be
so many people

The Sunday rush had begun. Lalaji was bustling about, welcoming customers, most of whom were also friends. October was a fine month. The weather was perfect. The cherry trees outside his shop were in full bloom. The tables full. The wedding season was around the corner. There'd be orders for a variety of goodies from his shop, there'd be catering to be done. He must look out for some young boys to help him, give him a hand. Perhaps that boy Aftab, the schoolteacher's son. He was a good boy, and the father would be pleased to have his son busy.

Ah! Here was Sardar Manjit Singh now, along with his family. There were other Sikh families heading this way. The gurudwara prayers would be over and everyone was en route for the famous paneer-puri with alu and special chai. It was a regular Sunday lunch here. After a quick shout to Chottu to move his lazy bones to wipe the tables and get the plates shining 'Onthedoubleonthe double!' Lalaji beamed, rushing, open-armed, towards the Manjit Singh family, especially Badi Beeji. He was not disappointed. They were immediately deep in discussion about the size of the laddoos that were to be sent out with the invitations for Harpreet's wedding. Little Angad squeezed his way between Beeji and Lalaji, begging for the laddoos to be besan ones rather than motichoor. He tugged at their arms; at whatever bit of clothing he could get his hands on.

'Chal huth,' Beeji gave him a surprisingly hard shove. Lalaji, too happy to see anyone in distress, soothed the child with the promise of a free besan-ka-laddoo right now, since they were still hot and fresh.

The crowds were accommodated, the food served, hot and chatpatta, when Lalaji saw the schoolmaster's son hesitate outside the shop, school bag heavy across his shoulders. In a generous, benevolent mood, he waved his ample arms and called out, 'Aao putter, you've been angry with me, no, my son? You haven't come in for your favourite tikkis and samosas – kyon? Don't be angry, beta. I'm like your father, no? And fathers must protect their sons, no? Aao na, why're you being so shy? Bhai, you're not the bridegroom here, Harpreet putter is, kyon?' The first part of the speech had been in the boy's ear, the second said loudly enough to draw the desired burst of laughter from the gathering. The bridegroom-to-be looked suitably sheepish and Aftab hung his head too.

'Aao bache, see, here's your little friend to whom I've promised a garama garam laddoo – here, there's one for you too.'

Angad scooted over to an already crowded bench and pulled his friend down next to him. 'Why're you carrying your school bag on a Sunday, Afti – not planning to top our class are you?'

He looped an arm about his shoulder and held his laddoo out to Aftab. 'Cheers!' he said, biting into it as though sipping whiskey.

'Stupid,' hissed Aftab, trying not to be drawn into the general warm friendliness that pervaded the space. It was too hot. Too close. He wanted to run away. There were too many people. There shouldn't have been so many. He hadn't thought there'd be so many people. He wasn't prepared for this. He couldn't. He couldn't.

'So dost, still brooding like a hen, I see. Look, I'm giving you twenty-four hours to stop thinking you're some Hrithik Roshan. Just twenty-four hours, and then I'm going back to that Major uncle, okay?' Angad hissed into Aftab's ear. Aftab stiffened, tried to control his thumping heart.

'Here,' said Angu, 'Now get comfortable, enjoy your laddoo – you want a cold drink? Here, take this silly bag off – oof what've you got in here?'

Angu began opening the bag to check the contents. 'Leave it!' Aftab barked. It came out louder than he'd intended. People turned to look as he held the bag. The bag. Lalaji was coming towards him.

'Aftab …?'

He came towards him, arms outstretched. He was going to take the bag, open it. But Aftab wasn't ready, he wasn't ready yet. But he must ….

But then there came the sound of a jeep roaring. Lalaji turned to look. There was some commotion outside. A jeep roaring away. Screeching. Shouts – Stop! Stop them! Roaring away. The crowded shop emptied in seconds, leaving Aftab blinking, his finger poised on 'the detonator'. Relief flooded him. He'd been saved. They'd all been saved. Relief swamped him.

'Is he dead?'

'Who is it?'

'It's a firangi.'

'Could it be the same firangi?'

'Yes, yes, it is the same fellow.'

'Someone call the police.'

Aftab is drawn out, still clutching the bag to his chest. 'There's a body been thrown from a jeep.' Angu's voice is high, like an excited girl's. 'Come look.' He pulls his friend forward into the thickening crowd. They squeeze through.

And there, sprawled, beaten, broken. Akram.

'Akram Bhai!' the whisper is hoarse – a whimper.

'Who?' asks Angu.

'Akram! My Akram Bhai – they've killed my Akram Bhai!'

He's beyond caution now, beyond caring. He doesn't care who knows – he's through with his lies and his denials.

He kneels next to the body. 'Akram Bhai,' he can barely get the words out from his tear-choked throat. Akram Bhai. The crowd leans in closer. And Aftab, with tears blinding his eyes, finds the button and draws the string. Just as Akram Bhai has taught him.

There's no time for him to get away.

22

The dead are dead

She kneels next to her son's body and keens. There's not much left of him. But she caresses the hand that just yesterday massaged the ache from her feet. Who will release the pain from her heart now?

Her husband sits beside her, near their son's head. His mind has vultures in it. Did I do enough? Should I have beaten him more? Less? Why didn't I know? What didn't I know?

Amir sits at his brother's feet. Holding on to them. He should have held on before. When Boey refused to take him on his adventures, he should have held on, then. Maybe he could have prevented this?

Shazia gets up. She cannot bear the little helpless animal sounds escaping from her mother. She tries to find some relief outside. But she can feel all eyes on her. She goes to the wall where she had sat with her little Boey and the merry Angu. She's torn into pieces. Her brother is gone. So is her husband. Both have died horrible, violent deaths. She misses her Akram, mourns him. But, at the same time, she is furious with him. He knew. He knew that he'd be sending the child to his death. Her brother. He knew. And that's why he wanted to see him alone at night. He knew that she wouldn't have allowed it. Ever. How had he convinced his shagirdh? The same way as he'd convinced her to use her body to free Feroze Bhai? Had he not told Aftab the whole truth? Had he told him that he'd get away? Oh Aftab, Aftab, my brother. I'm sorry. I'm sorry that I let you go alone. She hugs herself. Akram. She hears keening, her mother inside the house. How will she tell them? Can they take more pain? She strokes her belly. Crying that she never managed to tell her husband. That there was a little life that grew within her. His life. Hers – theirs. What will she do now? Where will she go? She knows now that she doesn't want her child to choose the path of violence. She couldn't bear it. Peace. All she wants is peace. She is so alone.

They are so alone. Yes, there are people here with them. But many of their friends, neighbours – Abbu's colleagues – have not come. For they are at funerals of their own. The entire city is in mourning today. And their dead are dead because of Aftab. The invitation cards arrived at the Manjit Singh household to be met by an entire family of corpses. The whole clan nearly wiped out. There are more dead than living. There's not a dry eye in the city today. Priests, pundits, gyanis and mullahs are overworked, preparing for last rites.

And the dead are dead because of Aftab.

It is time. As Aftab's body is lifted, a cry goes up – he's just a child, a child. Too young yet to be received by the earth. He's carried out of the door. What little is left of him. The mother's heart is breaking, although there is nothing left to break. *My sonmysonmysonmyson*. She cannot bear the finality of this parting. Oh my son.

She comes out into the sunlight. Distraught, despairing. Someone pulls her away. The body must be allowed to go on its journey.

And at the gate she sees another woman's grieving face. She hesitates. She is burdened by her sorrow. And now, with this new arrival, she is also burdened with despairing guilt. It's because of her son that the other has come to this gate – hair undone, dressed in white.

Then there are jeeps and wailing sirens. The army men have arrived, Major Ramneeq. Others. Their weapons holstered, but there. In case. In case … on the other side, the streets are filling up with people from the town. Young men, with weapons of their own. As the bodies are brought out, they raise their rifles and fire into the air. Instinctively, the hands of the military men are drawn to their own weapons.

The sound shakes Ammi out of her deep, dark place. 'No!' she shouts, 'No!!' she commands, rushing forward. 'No,' knocking the weapons right out of the men's hands.

'No! There will be no guns. There will be no guns at my son's funeral.

'No more guns – please no more guns.'

They look at each other. Aftab's mother. Angad's mother. Each shedding tears for just – dead sons. Has she come to share grief? Or to accuse? Blame?

Ammi takes a step forward. And Angad's mother comes forward too. They stop. They look only at each other as their sons are taken away.

There will be time to close the space between them.

There will be time to heal.

AFTERWORD

She rocks herself, hugging herself. Back and forth. Back and forth. Her tiny, newborn son held close to her, tight in her embrace. Holding him now, now that the violence is done and all that connected her to it is gone. And all those who were her link with it are gone. She hugs her son, her sleeping son. Let him sleep. Sleep. He is the only one who sleeps nowadays. The only one who wakes and smiles, refreshed, happy to see his mother's solemn face. His grandmother's, which squeezes smiles out of her barren heart so that he will know what a smile looks like.

The emerald in Shazia's eyes has faded, her cheeks are drawn, the mouth drooping with too much sorrow. Her son flutters his long dark lashes and opens his clear eyes to meet hers. There is wisdom in those baby eyes. There is a question.

Will I follow in my father's footsteps?

A shudder jolts Shazia and life seeps back into her eyes. Colour rushes into her cheeks as the blood starts to flow. 'Will he follow in his father's footsteps?'

'No!' she sits up, straightens her long-bent back, squares her stooping shoulders. No.

Her son, her precious, precious son will not, will not ever hold a gun in his tender hands. His feet will never walk the killer's path. His father's path.

'Never!' she breathes out loud now.

'There will be no guns at my son's funeral.'

'Whatever else happens,
let there be peace.'

– *a girl from Baramullah*